NO ONE TO TRUST

ROCKFORD SECURITY MYSTERY SERIES

L. A. DOBBS

1
____

*F*ree. *I'm finally free.*

Chase Evans walked out of the Southern Nevada Correctional Facility and into the chilly early-October sunshine. Funny how freedom felt an awful lot like being alone. Not that he'd expected anyone to show up for his release. Especially not Shane. Hell, his brother hadn't visited him for months now and their last phone conversation had been over a week ago. Still, things were a universe away from when he'd entered the prison. Half a decade behind bars did that to a guy.

Not that he regretted his decision. Not for a second.

Collar turned up on his frayed denim jacket, Chase shoved his hands into the pockets of his faded jeans.

With nothing better to do inside, he'd worked out like a fiend, gotten into the best physical shape of his life, even splurged on a few tats to go with his tough, new attitude.

If people were going to assume he was some kind of badass, he figured he might as well look the part. Yesterday, he'd had his thick brown hair buzz cut super short at the prison barber shop by a dude serving twenty years for grand larceny. He'd skipped the shave though. Stubble felt right these days. Made him look less fresh-faced kid and more hardened criminal. Not to mention the persona had saved him from a severe beating more than once behind bars.

He kept his head down and his eyes lowered as he strode across the asphalt tarmac toward the bus hut in the distance. With luck, he wouldn't have to wait long for the next shuttle back to Las Vegas.

Sin City. The sin part was certainly right.

He'd paid dearly for those sins, even if they were someone else's.

The dry desert wind whistled loud in his ears, and he hunched farther down into his jacket. Now that he was out, he had to find some way to support himself, get a new place to live, maybe a car or a motorcycle once he'd earned enough cash. Only trouble was, not too many people wanted to hire ex-cons, and his brief stint of college education wouldn't help him much now.

Honestly. Who the heck wanted to pay an attorney who couldn't even keep themselves out of the slammer?

No one. That's who.

It figured his dreams of practicing law had fizzled, just like the rest of his shitfest of a past. The sacrifices he'd made might've been noble, but they sure hadn't done him or—if his younger brother's recent attitude was any indication—anyone else any good.

"You look like you could use a ride."

Chase froze. The deep male voice came from his left. His gut clenched at the familiar tone, cool and slightly sarcastic. Blake Rockford. The last person he'd expected to see again.

Last he knew, the guy had retired from the Las Vegas Police Department and started his own security firm. He and Blake had worked some part-time security jobs together before Chase had gone off to law school and Blake had joined the force. Chase had even been willing to take a bullet for the guy once upon a time during a botched attempted robbery.

Too bad his hero days were long gone now.

He glanced up and saw Blake looking as GQ as he remembered, in his crisp suit and mirrored aviator shades. Not even the steady breeze dared ruffle the guy's short, dark hair. Blake looked like he'd walked off of some espionage movie set.

Chase himself? Not so much.

Listless and exhausted beyond his thirty-five years, Chase sighed and shook his head, his voice low and monotone. "What do you want, man?"

"I want to talk to you." Blake pushed away from the side of a navy blue sedan and crossed his arms. "I have a job proposition for you."

"A job?" Chase scoffed. "What kind of a job could you possibly have for me?"

"You know I run my own security firm now, right?"

Chase didn't answer, just stared at the man who used to be his closest friend, the man he hadn't spoken a word to since he'd entered prison. Not that Blake hadn't tried to contact him. But Chase couldn't. He just couldn't.

The guy reminded him of everything he'd lost.

"I want you to come work for me," Blake said, slipping off the sunglasses so Chase could see the sincerity in his piercing blue eyes. That stare—nicknamed The Hurt—had caused many a woman to swoon back in the day, and many a crook to soil his shorts.

"Me?" He snorted. "You must be nuts, man. In case

you haven't noticed, I just walked out of a goddamned prison. I'm hardly security firm material."

"You're wrong, Chase. You're exactly what I need."

"For what? A janitor? No thanks." He straightened to his full six-foot height and squared his shoulders, making himself as large and intimidating as possible. Another useful tool he'd learned inside. "I'm not interested."

Blake didn't blink an eye. "Cut the poor-me attitude, all right? You got a shitty deal in that trial, no doubt about it. But now you're back in the real world and you deserve another chance, Chase. I'm here to offer you one. I need a bodyguard for the Bryants, the owners of the Lucky Ace Hotel and Casino. All my other guys are out on assignment and I need someone I can trust. Are you in?"

"What makes you think you can trust me?"

"Other than the fact you saved my life?"

"Whatever, man," Chase said, shrugging off the accolade. "It wasn't like that."

"Considering I had the barrel of a Glock 9mm two inches from my nose before you blindsided the guy, knocked the weapon from his hand, and took a bullet in the process, I'd say it was exactly like that." Blake stepped closer, several inches taller and broader than Chase despite his added muscle. "Jeez. Lawyers. You want to stand here and argue about the past or get on with your future?"

The reminder of his previous career aspirations stung. He'd loved the law and had envisioned a future for himself defending the underprivileged. Fighting the good fight, like some kind of cape-wearing, Justice League, court-appointed superhero.

God. What a naïve bastard I was.

Time and circumstances and even his own family had taken his dreams and run them through the shredder. No Hallmark moments there. Not like the Rockfords. He remembered spending time with Blake and his large, happy clan when they'd worked together. He'd thought families like that only existed in movies or fairy stories for kids, but no. The Rockfords were the real thing—genuine, gigantic, and generous to a fault. They looked out for one another, took care of one another.

His chest ached with want for what he'd never had, what he'd never have now that he'd screwed up his life. Sighing, he shifted his feet and rubbed a hand over his face.

Dammit.

It wasn't like opportunities were knocking down his door, but this felt too easy.

Too right, if he was honest. These days, right

scared him. Right had gotten him into this whole mess in the first place. He met Blake's steely gaze direct. "What about my criminal record? Most folks aren't keen on having an ex-con guard anything valuable, especially their lives."

"The Bryants trust my judgment. If I vouch for you, they won't question it." Blake arched one dark brow and gave Chase a visual once-over. "What? You got a better offer waiting?"

No. I got zero offers waiting.

When Chase didn't answer, Blake continued. "Listen, I'll pay you good money, which you can use to save up for a place of your own. Can't have you sleeping on my sofa forever."

"Your sofa?" Chase crossed his arms. "I'm staying at a halfway house. It's part of my parole."

"Not anymore." Blake stared Chase down. "I talked to your parole officer and worked it out. If you take my job offer, you can stay with me until you find your own place."

Chase did his best not to squirm under the intense scrutiny. Blake had been a good friend once, and people weren't exactly lining up to hire him. How the guy would be as a boss, he didn't know, but it couldn't be any worse than some of those sadistic asshole prison guards.

Besides, it wouldn't be forever. If he didn't like it, he could always move into the halfway house and find other employment. Not to mention the fact he didn't have to hide his background from Blake. The guy knew almost all there was to know about him—the good, the bad, and the downright heinous.

"Fine." Chase exhaled and stared out into the endless desert landscape surrounding them. Nothing but dust and cactus and desolation as far as the eye could see. Beneath the blazing sun, the asphalt had warmed quickly and now shimmered with heat. "When do I start?"

"Now." Blake grinned, all white teeth and confidence. He jabbed a button on his key fob and the locks on the car doors clicked open. "Get in. I'll give you the details on the way to my house."

2

———

Two days later, Chase walked into the Lucky Ace Hotel and Casino on Fremont Street. The place reeked of Old Vegas charm—burgundy leather chairs and matching solid burgundy carpet, green felt card tables, faux chandeliers and twinkle lights on the ceiling to mimic a starry sky.

He futzed with his suit jacket for the umpteenth time then straightened his tie. He felt like a trained monkey in this getup he'd borrowed from Blake's closet, but his new boss insisted on professional dress for this particular assignment. Chase gazed around the area, searching for the information desk. His meeting was supposed to be with Warren Bryant, the hotel's owner, and Owen Rockford, Blake's cousin and head of security for the Lucky Ace's casino floor.

Now, if he could just find their offices he'd be all set.

Before he took another step, an attractive, dark-haired woman who looked about Chase's age approached him from the left. Dripping with jewels and designer duds, it appeared she could buy and sell the place twenty-times over.

"Are you the new bodyguard?" Her voice could have frozen an eskimo. She assessed him from head to toe with a possessive green gaze, her eyes heavily lined and mascaraed. "Hmm. I suppose you'll do. I'm Katherine Bryant, by the way."

She held out a perfectly manicured hand for him to shake.

"Chase Evans. And yeah." He coughed and did his best not to stare at the way her low-cut sweater showed off all her assets. "Yes, I mean. I'm the new bodyguard."

"Good." She slid her pricey handbag over her arm and waved for him to follow her out the door. "Hurry up. I've got a lot of errands to get done today. I need to hit Neiman's and Barney's and Chanel, if there's time. Then there's my appointment at the salon this after-noon and—"

"Um." Chase dug in his heels despite her decisive commands. "I'm supposed to be meeting with your husband and the head of casino security in a few minutes."

"What?" She gave him an irritated look, then a dismissive wave. "Oh, don't worry about them. I'll just text Warren and let him know you're with me."

As she pulled out her phone and thumbed in a quick text, Chase took a deep breath. He was thankful to Blake for the job, really he was, but the last thing he wanted to do these days was babysit some rich airhead with diamond baguettes for brains.

"Okay." Katherine shoved her phone back in her bag and hailed the doorman over to summon her car. Moments later a sleek black Bentley swerved up to the curb and Chase found himself ensconced in rich leather and pure luxury. Hell, this ride was probably worth more than his entire life thus far. The thought made his flagging hopes for his new position shrink even more. Blake had talked up the job, made it sound like a fresh start, a way to make a new name for himself, a chance to begin again. But from the looks of things now, the only thing he'd be called for the foreseeable future was glorified nanny to the somewhat rich and almost famous.

The next few hours passed in a blur of endless racks of clothing and shoes and purses. Then came the salon. If the barbers back in prison could've seen this racket, they'd have creamed their shorts. Jesus, they even served him top-shelf champagne while he waited for her royal highness—as he'd come to think of Katherine already.

Not that he'd slack on his duties, of course. He'd remain vigilant during his boredom, keeping an eye out for any suspicious lurkers or potential danger.

Finally, primped and teased to within an inch of her life, he and his new assignment made their way back to the Lucky Ace in the rarified world of the Bentley. She sat on one end of the long bench seat while he occupied the opposite corner, staring silently out the window. Small talk had never been his strong suit, and now... Well, now that he had a record, he couldn't imagine anyone would care what he had to say anyway, so he kept his mouth shut.

Not that he had to worry about dead air. Katherine hadn't shut up once since they'd headed back to the hotel. She rambled on endlessly about her new purchases, then gossiped about her friends who Chase had never met and didn't want to after the awful things she'd said about them. Mostly though, she ranted about her neglectful husband and how he didn't pay any attention to her anymore. Considering Chase now worked for the guy, he didn't want to hear anymore. Maintaining his distance was crucial to protecting these people. If he got too close to any of them he couldn't stay objective. And he had to stay objective.

People's lives might depend on it.

The car pulled up to the hotel and Katherine exited, leaving Chase to deal with her trunkful of purchases. Laden with bags hanging from each arm and boxes piled high enough to obscure his vision, he followed her inside the Lucky Ace then to a private elevator in a secluded hallway near where the corporate offices were located. Despite his full arms, he managed to look over and spot Warren Bryant's office a short distance away in the secluded hallway. Good to know, for future reference. The elevator dinged and they climbed on board for the short ride to the Bryant's private condo on the top floor of the hotel.

From over the top of the boxes he gazed around the condo's interior and thought it fit Katherine to a T —sleek, modern, and edgy. The dark color scheme of grays, blues, and browns was interrupted here and there by a splash of white and he wondered briefly if that's why Warren Byrant left his wife alone so much —did she try to dominate him like she dominated their interior design?

"Thank you so much for bringing all of these in," Katherine said, tossing her designer bag onto a side table then directing him to follow her down the hall and into a spacious master suite with a large attached travertine-tiled bathroom. "Just toss them on the chaise over there, please. You are such a sweetheart."

Her tone turned low and husky, so sticky sweet it made Chase's teeth ache. He did as she asked, then turned and straightened his tie once more. "Well, okay then, Ms. Bryant. I guess I should get back downstairs so I can have my meeting with Mr. Bryant."

"What's your hurry?" Her full lips curved downward into a pout and she stepped closer. "I was hoping we could get to know each other better."

Chase did his best not to sneeze as the heavy, cloying scent of her spicy perfume tickled his nose. From the gleam in her eye and the finger she traced over his jaw and down his neck, she wasn't inviting him to afternoon tea. *Shit.* He took a deep breath and stepped away. "I'm sorry, ma'am, but I have other obligations."

"Ma'am?" She winked and once more closed the small distance between them, pressing her generous curves against him. "Aren't you just too adorable?"

Her wandering hand traced down his chest and toyed with his tie before returning to cup the back of his neck. His posture stiffened. He hated people touching the back of his neck, reminded him too much of the way his mom used to punish him when he was growing up.

Katherine apparently mistook his revulsion for hesitation because the fingers at his nape drifted upward into his hair, her long nails stroking and massaging his scalp, scratching hard enough to hurt as she leaned in to whisper into his ear. "Relax. My husband won't mind. We're separated."

He didn't want this, didn't want her. She wasn't his type at all. Katherine was too forward, too demanding, too high-maintenance for his taste. He wanted someone sweet and kind and generous to warm his lonely bed at night. But he also didn't want to lose his job, especially not on the first day, and he was pretty sure sleeping with the client's wife, whether they were really separated or not, was not in his job description.

Chase placed his hands on her shoulders and attempted to move her aside. "This isn't right, Ms. Bryant."

"Maybe not, but being bad is so much more fun." Before Chase knew what was happening, Katherine's hands skimmed down his flat belly to cup his crotch. The movement startled him and she must have taken the jerk of his hips as a 'yes'. She wrapped her lacquered nails around his belt and tugged pulling it free from his trousers. "I can make you feel so good, Chase. Let me make you feel good."

She reached for the closure on his waistband, but he caught her hand in his. Katherine seemed like the vindictive type. She'd probably complain to Blake if he didn't do as she wanted, maybe even accuse *him* of coming on to *her*. Maybe Blake would believe her and fire him, but that didn't matter. Screwing around with someone else's wife was just wrong and besides, even after five years of celibacy in prison, he was not the least bit tempted to get in the sack with Katherine. He found her repulsive.

She tried to kiss him, melting herself against him. He managed to avoid her lips and set her aside.

"I have to go. Sorry." He headed for the front door like his ass was on fire. "Goodbye, Ms. Bryant."

Chase didn't wait for her response, just jabbed the elevator buttons until the door slid open then jammed them again to get the damned thing to close once he'd boarded. It wasn't until he'd reached the lobby once more that he realized he'd left his belt behind in her condo, but by that point he didn't care. If Mr. Bryant found it and fired him, so be it.

He should've known this job was too good to be true.

Guys like him didn't get second chances.

Guys like him didn't deserve them.

———

BY SEVEN-THIRTY THAT NIGHT, Chase had worked himself into a fine snit. As he sat on the sofa in the living room of Blake's two-story modern home in the upscale suburb of Summerlin, staring at the muted TV, images from the local news flickered by. He'd racked his brain for hours thinking of a way to explain his earlier behavior at Katherine Bryant's condo to Blake.

There was no way in hell she hadn't reported the incident to Rockford Security by now, and he'd be looking for a new job come morning. Didn't matter he hadn't done anything wrong. Didn't matter she'd probably lied and told Blake *he'd* assaulted *her*. Didn't matter this had been his best, last shot at normal.

All that mattered in this world was power and prestige and money.

Chase had learned that the hard way.

A key scraped in the lock on the front door and Chase's posture stiffened, his chest tight and his throat dry. He closed his eyes and took a deep breath, his fight or flight instincts fully engaged. He might be on the loser backend of this busted ride, but that didn't mean he would go down without a fight.

Soon, Blake stepped around the corner from the foyer into the living room and Chase shot to his feet, rushing into his explanation before his boss could say a word.

"Look, man. I'm really sorry about what happened earlier. I know I should've reacted differently." He stopped, faltered, scowled. "No, actually. I don't really have any idea how I should've reacted in that situation. But I know it's your name and your company on the line, and I—"

Blake held up a hand and shook his head. "Don't worry about it. It's fine."

"What?" Chase took a step back and scrubbed a hand through his hair. "Fine? Really? You mean you *want* me to sleep with Katherine Bryant?"

"Huh?" Blake looked as stunned as Chase felt. "What? No! Wait, don't tell me you had sex with her. What the hell, Chase?"

"Heck no, man." He rubbed his eyes. "I mean, she put the moves on me, but I said no and got the hell out of there, man. I haven't slept with anyone."

"Good. Then you haven't ruined your chances."

"Chances for what?"

"Chances that I can place you with the right—"

Blake glanced from Chase to the tv then grabbed the remote from the coffee table and turned up the volume. On screen a reporter stood outside the Lucky Ace Casino while red and blue lights flashed in the background.

"Tragedy struck tonight at the Lucky Ace Casino when Owner Warren Bryant was found dead in his office ... a victim of an apparent homicide ..."

Chase's anxiety went into overdrive. Warren Bryant, the client whose body he was supposed to be guarding was dead? He slumped back down on the sofa while Blake took a seat next to him.

Onscreen, the reporter's mouth was still moving, but Chase wasn't listening. He was too busy berating himself. He should have been there. It was his job to protect the family and he'd screwed up. He'd been embarrassed about running out after his confrontation with Katherine, but that was one thing. No one had gotten hurt. But this was serious. Way more serious. A man was dead on his watch.

The tv flipped from the talking head to a video clip. Chase recognized the dimly lit interior of the hallway where he had bolted from the private elevator hours before, hell bent on escaping Katherine Bryant and her erotic overtures. The door to Warren Bryant's office lurked near the edge of the frame, his name twinkling in gold metallic letters against the wood like a cheerful obituary.

Chase sucked in a breath as an all-too-familiar figure darted out of the elevator then out of frame, never once revealing their face to the camera. Per the reporter, the clip was time stamped only moments before Bryant's body was discovered.

Crap.

Talk about being in the wrong place at the wrong ass time.

Chase's stomach lurched as he realized what the video meant. A few minutes ago he'd been worried about getting fired and losing Blake's trust over fleeing Katherine Bryant's advances, but now his hasty retreat had resulted in something much worse. Because, by the way the reporter on tv was talking, he was now the number one suspect in Warren Bryant's murder.

BLAKE SIGHED and hung his head. "Please tell me that isn't you."

Chase exhaled long and slow, his attention focused on his stockinged feet. "I swear to God I didn't kill anyone."

"I know that."

Chase rushed into an explanation. "I was running away from Katherine! She came onto me and I just had to get out of there. And now it's my fault Warren Bryant is dead."

"It's not your fault because you didn't kill him," Blake said. "I can't blame you for running out, Katherine's a viper. She tried to come on to me once, too. Does it to everyone, I think."

"But if I had kept my head and stayed at my post, I might have prevented the client's murder." Chase's shoulders slumped. Blake had trusted him with this bodyguard assignment and he'd screwed up the first day.

SILENCE LOOMED between them as the newscast moved on to an upcoming concert by local gal turned worldwide country superstar, Jan Winters. Chase felt as useless as tits on a bull, but he needed to know, needed to plan for a future that grew darker by the second. "I'm fired, aren't I?"

"What?" Blake gave him an annoyed look. "No. Of course not. I would never do that to you. But maybe we should, you know, wait a bit for this whole thing to die down before I send you on another assignment. Have you lay low while the cops find the real killer and all."

"Right." Chase flopped back against the sofa cushions and scrubbed his hands over his face. "Pretty sure that's just a fancy way of saying I'm off the payroll. I don't blame you. I'll call my parole officer tonight and move to the halfway house tomorrow. Thanks for letting me crash here for the past couple of nights anyway. It was worth a shot, right?"

He pushed to his feet and headed toward the bathroom.

"Dammit, Chase. Since when did you give up so easily, huh?"

Blake's words halted him in his tracks. Back in prison, someone calling him a coward would've landed them in traction. But Blake was his friend. The guy had put his ass and his company name on the line to give him a shot at a better life. Not to mention the fact that Blake was right. Chase was running away and admitting it to himself damned near killed him.

He wasn't a quitter. He didn't run from his problems, he solved them.

Blake stood and walked over to him. "Listen. You can still work for me, just in a different capacity, okay? We'll find something for you to do in the office. My sister Olivia's always complaining about needing help with all the paperwork. With your law background, that should be right up your alley."

Chase held back a defeated sigh through sheer force of will. Pushing mountains of forms and files would be even worse than playing caretaker to the rich and spoiled. Even in law school, all the paperwork had been his least favorite part. Honestly, it would be a fate worse than prison. Still, it would guarantee him steady work while he figured out what to do with the rest of his godforsaken life.

"Fine," he agreed at last, his tone dejected and his shoulders stooped.

"Good." Blake slapped him on the back and handed him a credit card then headed upstairs. "Order some pizza while I take a shower. I'm starving."

Chase stared at the plastic in his hand before shuffling back into the living room and picking up the phone and a nearby menu. Blake's switch in his job duties might not be ideal, but the fact the guy had handed him a credit card with a limit most likely higher than the national budget of Switzerland without blinking an eye meant Blake trusted him.

And trust was a precious commodity in Chase's world these days.

He vowed then and there to do whatever was necessary to keep it.

3

Chase had lain awake all night waiting for the police to come and arrest him, but they never did. Maybe they'd gotten a lead on the real killer and this nightmare would soon be over. He could only hope. In the morning, he dressed and went to his new assignment at Rockford Security.

His small desk was situated in one corner of the large, open-concept Rockford Security offices. He sat there now, staring at a mound of paperwork waiting for him to sort and file. His white button-down shirt pulled at the shoulders, his tie felt too tight, and the loafers he'd borrowed from Blake pinched his toes. For one brief moment he considered chucking it all and heading straight for the halfway house where he belonged.

Then he remembered all the support Blake had shown him since he'd walked out of the prison, a few days prior. No one else had cared about him or his future, except Blake Rockford. Even when he'd run out of the casino, Blake had believed him that he was fleeing Katherine and had nothing to do with her husband's murder. He owed the guy, even if it meant feeling like a tricked out baboon's ass stuck in cubicle hell.

"I expected to find you at the Lucky Ace today."

Chase looked up to find Laura Rockford, Blake's youngest sister, leaning one hip against the side of his desk. From her narrowed hazel eyes and knowing expression, she had a pretty good idea something was up with him. And given the fact she was a journalist with Las Vegas's largest newspaper, he wasn't about to spill any more details than necessary. He'd learned just how brutal and conniving the press could be during his trial. Not that he cast the same shadow over Laura, but he couldn't be too careful these days. "Yeah. There was... a problem."

Laura lifted her chin in a slight nod. "Problem, huh? That's kind of why I expected you there. You know, to clear your name and all?"

"Blake told you about the footage." It wasn't a question. He looked up at her through his lashes, steeling himself against the condemnation he was sure to find in her gaze. Instead, he only found intense interest—and something more. Something he'd never expected to see again. Not in this lifetime anyway.

Compassion.

Chase shook his head and remained silent.

Laura pushed a stack of files aside and settled atop the corner of his desk. "So there's DNA evidence too, huh?"

"What?"

"I just came from the police station and one of my friends on the force said they collected some of your hairs from the bedroom in the Bryant's condo. What's up with that?" She pursed her lips and tapped her index finger against her bottom lip, appearing to think deeply about this though her tone said it was all an act. "Were you and Katherine uh..." Laura made a gesture with her hands. "Doing the horizontal tango."

"What? No!" Chase pushed his chair back from the desk and crossed his arms. Memories of Katherine snagging her claws in his hair surfaced. She must have pulled some out. "I did *not* sleep with that woman. No way."

"Hmm." She assessed him with a suspicious gaze. "Seems odd that a bodyguard would be needed in his client's bedroom. Troy, my detective friend, said they even found a few on the bed itself, on the pillows." She shrugged then studied her fingernails. "Then there's the belt, of course."

Shit.

Chase pressed his fingers into his now pounding temples and closed his eyes. With his past sins, he shouldn't be surprised no one believed him, but that didn't make the accusations hurt any less. Then again, it didn't really matter what the truth was once you'd been painted with the felony brush. All that constitutional innocent-until-proven-guilty jargon he'd studied in law school was nothing but a crock of shit. "Listen, I swear I didn't have sex with her. She came on to me. After I declined her offer, I got the hell out of there. That's when the cameras near the elevators caught me on tape. End of story."

He'd done his best to keep his voice down, but from the way the other employees were eyeballing him and Laura, he'd failed miserably.

Laura leaned closer and whispered, "What about the rumpled bed and vaginal fluid they found on the sheets?"

"What? That wasn't from me!" He held her gaze despite the fact his heart felt like it would beat out of his chest. How did the sheets get rumpled? Did Katherine have another guy waiting in the wings or ...

"Wait a minute. What if she was trying to use me as an alibi. If she had something to do with Warren's death she'd want to have an alibi for the time of death."

"Now you're thinking properly." Laura gave him a slight wink. "If Katherine is involved, she probably arranged for someone to do it for her. She doesn't exactly seem the type that would enjoy blood on her freshly manicured hands."

"Wow." Chase couldn't suppress a small, impressed smile. "You're pretty good at your job."

"Damn straight." Pride flashed across her pretty face. "I'm the one who broke the huge story about the serial killer framing Mike McQuade."

"Who?" Chase gave her a confused stare, nose scrunched. "Sorry. I've been out of the loop for a while."

"He owns a gaming company called M Cubed. Guess it all started after you were convicted."

Right. Still hard to grasp sometimes that the world had carried on without him while he'd been locked away behind bars. So much had changed, so much was gone. He tamped down the familiar ache of loneliness and regret in his chest. Wouldn't do any good to dwell on the past. Not anymore. What was done was done. Time to move on.

Laura straightened and adjusted the messenger

bag slung across her body. "Anyway. I'm trying to get the assignment from the Chronicle for Bryant's murder story, so I wanted to stop by and let you know I'll do what I can to deflect the heat off of you."

Stunned, he slumped back in his chair. "You'd do that for me?"

"Of course. Blake told me what you did for him on that security job, how you saved his life. We Rockfords owe you. Besides, now that you're working here that makes you practically one of us. And we take care of our own. Besides, I've crossed paths with Katherine and heard rumors. She's nasty so it's not too hard to think she'd try to set you up."

The Rockfords might be a bit flakey when it came to family, but hell if they weren't a loyal bunch. The fact that, other than Blake, they hardly knew him at all wasn't lost on Chase. In fact, it made their seeming acceptance and defense of him all the more astonishing.

"Thank you." He swallowed against the sudden pressure in his throat.

"No problem." She stood and headed for the exit. "I'll be in touch."

Chase watched her leave, a thought popping into his head. He pushed to his feet. "Hey, Laura."

"Yeah?" She walked back to him.

"If the police got my DNA from the hair, won't they want to question me?"

"Probably. But they'll have to get through Blake first. I'd say you've got a couple of hours before they bring you into the station."

Dread choked his breath and his pulse drummed loud in his ears. The last time the cops had dragged him into the station, he hadn't been a free man again for five years. Going back to prison now, after he'd just tasted life on the outside again, would kill him. Especially for another crime he didn't commit.

He couldn't do it. Not again. Not ever.

His inner turmoil must've shown on his face because Laura placed a comforting hand on his arm. "Don't worry. My friend Troy's assigned to the case. He's fair and open-minded, though a bit slow on the uptake sometimes." She laughed. "But he's an okay guy. He won't hold your record against you. Plus, there's a good chance the lead detective handling the murder is still tied up with Owen over at the casino. He's stalling her with a bogus search for the footage they need, but he can't hold her off forever."

"I was supposed to meet with Owen yesterday." He exhaled. "Before Katherine waylaid me."

"He's cool. He's got your back. We all do." Laura

squeezed his arm before heading out of the offices once more.

Overwhelmed, Chase sank back into his chair and toyed with his burgundy tie—another one of Blake's—while he considered his options. Having people stick their necks out to help him the way the Rockfords were, was completely foreign. Up until now, he'd been on his own. Even when it came to his brother, Shane.

Especially when it came to Shane.

Where the hell was his brother anyway? Shane still hadn't contacted him since he'd gotten out, despite the numerous texts and voicemails he'd left. He was starting to worry. His brother had never been the responsible type or a good judge of character. But still, if anything happened to him...

No. Chase pinched the bridge of his nose between his thumb and forefinger. He couldn't think like that. He had to focus on his most pressing issues now.

Clearing his name. Proving to the Rockfords he was worthy of their loyalty.

Then he could focus on Shane and all their history together.

A quick check of his watch showed it was close to eleven a.m. If Laura was right, he should have until mid-afternoon to do some digging on his own before the police showed up to haul him in for questioning.

He grabbed his denim jacket off the back of his chair and shrugged it on, his nose wrinkling at the flowery scent of fabric softener. Blake had washed all his stuff —all meaning the one outfit he currently owned— along with his own stuff the other night. Once he got back on his feet again, he definitely needed to go shopping for some new duds.

After checking to make sure Blake was busy in his office, Chase slipped into a nearby supply closet and snagged a pair of latex gloves, then ducked out a side entrance and headed for the bus hut on the corner to wait for the next shuttle to Fremont Street. He needed to find some scrap of evidence that proved his innocence before he faced the police. To go in with nothing would be too risky, given his current situation.

4

———

A short time later, Chase stepped off the bus in front of the Lucky Ace Hotel and Casino, surrounded by a small crowd of excited tourists and determined elderly who elbowed him out of the way in their rush to dump their latest social security checks into the awaiting slot machines.

He lingered behind for a few moments, spotting the squad car parked near the entrance. That female detective Laura had mentioned must still be there questioning Owen. Wary of being spotted lurking around the premises, he headed down the side of the building instead, toward one of the less busy entrances near the back.

Once inside, the cheerful clang of dropping coins and the smell of food wafting from the nearby food court helped to ease his nerves. With so many people inside, he should have sufficient cover to slip through the place unseen. Hopefully, anyway.

"Hey, aren't you the new guy at the office?"

Chase's heart stuttered at the words. So much for stealth.

He turned slowly and spotted a Rockford Security guard stationed near the door. *Play it cool. Play it cool. Play it cool.* He repeated the mantra over and over in his head, and he forced a smile as he stepped closer to the guy. "Yeah, that's me." He flashed his ID. "They sent me over to talk to Owen. Any idea where I might find him?"

"Probably still in his office with the police." The guard pointed toward the hall where Warren Bryant's office was located. "He's two doors down from the head honcho. Or ex-head honcho, I guess."

"Great. Thanks." Chase waved then headed off toward the private elevator where he'd ridden up to the condo with Katherine. A quick glance at the wall showed the traitorous security camera that had caught him bolting down the hall. *Dammit.* He should've noticed the security cameras there that first day, should've been more careful. Then again, he wasn't anticipating having to avoid being seen fleeing the scene of a murder.

Approaching the secluded hallway again, he lowered his head and pulled the collar of his jacket higher to obscure his face from any potential cops that might be snooping around. No mistakes this time. Just in and out and back to the offices to wait for the police like a good little suspect.

He had no idea what he was looking for. Maybe something in the condo that would incriminate Katherine? If he could even get in there. When he got to the elevator, however, a new idea struck. Careful to avoid detection, he headed a bit farther down and stopped at Warren Bryant's office door instead. The police were gone, apparently having completed their investigation of the murder scene. The area had been cordoned off with numerous strips of yellow police tape, but he wasn't about to let that stop him. If he could find a clue that cleared him in the office, he'd be golden.

Plan approved, he tugged on the latex gloves and reached for the handle, then halted, noticing the door was slightly ajar. From the hushed sound of rustling papers, someone was already in there. Adrenaline zinged through his system as his instincts went on high alert. Not a cop, since the police would leave the door wide open. So, who else? The real murderer?

He didn't have any weapons, but if worse came to

worse, he could bust out all of the hand-to-hand combat skills he'd learned in prison. Inmates might pull their punches inside when the warden was around, but outside in the Rec yard, it was no holds barred.

After a quick check of the area to make sure no one was watching him, he pushed the door open a bit farther and slipped inside through a large opening between two crisscrossed pieces of police tape. From across the room he spotted a woman, her platinum blond curls glistening beneath the overhead recessed lighting. Petite, curvy, and cute, she appeared to be on a fact-finding mission, given the way she was rifling through the drawers. The top of a large mahogany desk--squatting near the back of the spacious, elegantly appointed space—was empty, along with the bookshelves running the length of the wall behind it. Seemed all the contents of the room had already been taken into evidence by the police. Apparently this gal felt they'd left something behind though.

Chase quietly clicked the door shut behind him and scanned the space for security cameras. He didn't see any. Good. He could frisk the area without worrying about making another appearance on Candid Cop Camera.

The woman looked up at Chase as he *snicked* the

lock on the door into place. Her eyes were puffy and her nose was red, as if she'd been crying. An unwanted flare of sympathy spread through him, and he had the crazy urge to rush over and pull her into his arms. He tamped the crazy notion down deep and stepped closer, his voice low. "Who are you?"

She swiped a tangle of curls over her shoulder. "I'm Warren Bryant's daughter, Shelby. Who the hell are you?"

For a rich girl, she certainly wasn't dressed like one. In her simple jeans and plain T-shirt, she looked ready for a romp in the park or a walk on the beach, so different from the designer disaster he'd encountered with Katherine. She wore little makeup and her skin looked soft as silk. He clenched his hands at his sides to keep from reaching out and tracing a finger down her flawless cheek to confirm his hunch.

What the heck?

Here he was wasting his one opportunity to prove his innocence by ogling the casino boss's daughter. Who might possibly be the real killer here to remove evidence.

Her full lips thinned slightly and she squared her shoulders. She was several inches shorter than him, but refused to back down. He admired her bravery.

"I asked you who you were," she repeated, her tone

quiet and quavering. Not with fear though, if the spark in her eyes was any indication.

Chase stayed where he was, not wanting to spook her. "I'm with Rockford Security."

"Oh." Disappointment dampened the fire in her pretty blue eyes. "Marvelous. Lot of good you people did for my dad."

Affronted on behalf of his newfound benefactors and glad for the distraction, Chase defended his new employers. "Hey, we did the best we could. No one can plan for all contingencies."

"Contingencies?" Pink flushed her creamy cheeks and Chase amended his former statement. She wasn't just cute. She was beautiful. "Maybe this was just another job to you, but Dad was no contingency. And all because my stepmom's new bodyguard couldn't keep his goddamned pants zipped."

"Excuse me?" Outrage stormed Chase's system. "For the love of God, I did *not* sleep with that woman, okay?"

Shelby's eyes widened, her expression morphing from shock to anger. "You! You're the douchebag who slept with Katherine?"

"Did I lapse into Chinese? 'Cause I'm pretty certain I just said I didn't sleep with anyone." He did his best not to let his fury seep into his tone, but from the way she charged at him, he failed. *Get used to it, man.* People doubting his word would become par for the course these days now that he was officially an ex-con, but the fact she didn't believe him still rankled for some reason, dammit. "For the last freaking time. I. Did. Not. Sleep. With. Katherine. Bryant."

Shelby stepped up nose to nose with him--or nose to neck, given their height difference—and jabbed her finger into his chest. "Listen, asshole. I'm going to find out who killed my dad. And when I do, I'm going to take my time and savor ripping the bastard's balls off, nice and slow and infinitely painful. Understand?"

Chase gazed down at her, an odd admiration pounding through his veins. Her eyes blazed with conviction. She smelled of flowers and sweet redemption. At that moment he didn't think about his purpose for being in Warren Bryant's office or his criminal record or her threats against her father's murderer. In fact, at that moment all he could think about was Shelby Bryant.

HE SMELLED LIKE HEAVEN. Like sandalwood and soap and warm, clean male.

That was Shelby's first unwanted thought as she

got all up in the guy's grill. Odd, really, but then her entire life had been thrown topsy-turvy the past couple of days and grief over her dad's death had made her decidedly off-kilter.

With mere inches separating them now and her index finger pressed firmly against his hard chest, his heat enveloped her, seeped into her, warming the cold dark places her dad's murder had created. Which was bad. So very, very bad. This asshole could very well be responsible for her dad's death. Oh, she knew he hadn't actually done it. She'd seen the video of the man running out. She knew he'd been in the condo with Katherine. The timing wasn't right. He was probably just a dumb pawn in Katherine's game.

But he didn't *seem* dumb. Not like Katherine's usual boys. This one had an innocence to him, too. *Dammit*. She needed to focus on looking for clues, not being swayed by the hint of the tattoo that peeked out from beneath the left side of his starched shirt collar. Definitely not at how tall and broad he was or the sexy glint in his warm gray eyes.

No matter what this guy had or hadn't done, she didn't take Katherine's cast offs. For all she knew he was in here trying to obscure evidence at Katherine's request.

"And I didn't kill your father." His words emerged rough, deep, more growl than speech.

She didn't miss the way his gaze dropped to her lips before returning to her eyes.

No. This was ridiculous. She would not allow herself to be sidetracked. Not again. She would not allow herself to be the normal, quiet, gullible Shelby who always saw the bright side of life. The killing of her dad had changed all that overnight.

Shelby poked him hard once more, just for good measure. "Of course you'd say that."

"I said it because it's the truth." Each word grated past his firm lips like a curse. "Listen, lady. I just got out of prison, for Christ's sake. Why the hell would I want to go back?"

Well, *that* was a kicker. Shelby settled her weight onto her heels, increasing the space between them slightly. If she sprinted for it, she might make the door before him. Then again, given the power lurking in his long legs, maybe not. Her voice emerged more hesitant than she'd intended. "You were in prison?"

"Yes." The word seemed painful for him to say. "Not for murder though."

"Oh." She took another step back. "For what then? Mr.?"

"Evans. Chase Evans. And it was for drug trafficking." He shook his head and looked away. "It's a long story."

So much for distracting him with conversation. She eyed him up and down. "How'd you get a job with Rockford Security if you have a criminal record. Isn't there some kind of law against that?"

"No. No law. And Blake trusts me."

Well, I don't.

They stared at each other for a few beats and Shelby forced her tense shoulders to relax. "Why are you here?"

"I'm looking for evidence to prove I didn't kill your father." Chase kept his gaze focused on her as he said it, as if willing her to believe him. Under different circumstances, Shelby might have. After all, she was known for taking in strays. Men, animals. Hell, she even ran a local shelter for unwanted pets. And this guy certainly fit the feral bill—dark, dangerous, deeply wounded.

Shelby shook off her fanciful thoughts. Was he telling the truth? If so, he wasn't working with Katherine. She felt ridiculously relieved at the thought, but she wasn't about to trust the tall stranger. "Well, I'm sorry, but you can't be in here."

He snorted. "And you can? Last time I checked there was crime scene tape all over that doorway. This is where the murder took place, right? If so, then technically we're both contaminating a crime scene."

Her breath hitched at the mention of her dad's demise and tears welled in her eyes. *Shit.* The last thing she wanted to do was cry in front of this guy. It just hurt so damned bad. Like her heart had been ripped out. Despite her somewhat tenuous relationship with her father and all his nefarious deeds, she'd loved him deeply. He'd been the only family she'd had after her mom had walked out all those years ago.

She turned away and swiped her hand under her eyes. At least the place wasn't covered in blood and gore. The police hadn't said how he'd died when they'd called to inform her. Only that he was gone.

Gone. Dad's gone and I'm alone.

Stubbornness and grief bubbled inside her. "He was my family. I have every right to be here."

Cursing, Chase stormed past her and headed behind the desk. "Well, I'm not leaving until I get what I came for."

She winced as he yanked opened the same empty drawers she'd inspected minutes earlier. "There's nothing in there. I already looked."

"Well, I'm looking again." Chase bent and peered beneath the desk then laughed. "Huh, now what have we here?"

She joined him. "What?"

"Looks like a secret safe."

"Dad always said he had a hidden safe, but I never guessed it was under the desk..." Her father had mentioned keeping his most secret documents in the hidden safe and she'd been trying to figure out where it was during her search. Did Katherine know about it? If so she'd probably taken anything incriminating, but if not...

Chase had already ripped the rug aside and was frantically working the buttons trying to break the code.

"Stop that. You'll set off the alarm." Shelby pushed him aside. The contents of the safe wasn't any of this Neanderthal's business, but the way she saw it this might be her only chance to open it. She crouched and punched in a code her father had given her for one of the home safes years ago, praying he'd used the same one. Her birthday. The door *cha-chunked* open and they both squinted inside. "Do you see anything?"

"Just this." He reached past her and pulled out a plain manila folder. "Must be something important to lock it up like that." He flipped it open then whistled. "Nice."

Shelby stared at the paperwork he held. One packet was the prenuptial agreement Katherine had signed when she'd married Dad. The other was the Last Will and Testament of Warren Bryant. "So? Neither of those proves anything."

He perused the paperwork, glancing up at her from time to time before setting them aside and crossing his arms, his expression unreadable. "Tell me about your inheritance."

"Excuse me?"

"You inherit almost everything. Katherine gets only ten percent." Chase frowned down at the will. "It goes straight to you unless you are otherwise unable to inherit."

"What's that mean?" Shelby vaguely remembered her dad talking about protecting the casino. He'd worried about her sinking everything into her animal rescue business.

"It's an old clause, means if you become incapacitated somehow, unable to run the business normally." Chase glanced up at her. "Looks like you are perfectly capable of running the business normally."

"What are you talking about?" Mortified heat crept up her cheeks. Her dad had insisted she be his beneficiary, but she didn't care at all about his dirty money or his casino. "I don't like what you're implying."

"And what exactly is that?"

"That I killed my dad to get my inheritance."

"Did you?"

"Hell. No."

"Well, neither did I."

Shelby frowned. "What about that prenup? Katherine certainly had motive. She's wanted out for years but wouldn't get much if she divorced him."

Chase picked up the file again. "According to these, she'd get even less if he died."

Hot tears stung Shelby's eyes again and she sniffled despite herself. "I don't want my dad's money. I just want him back." Angry at Chase for interrupting her search and angry at herself for breaking down in front of him, she lashed out. "Just go. Get out of here before I alert the police."

He left without another word.

5

———

Chase stared across the worn wooden table at the detective questioning him. He'd been stuck in this dingy little room for over an hour already and this woman had finally decided he was worth her precious time to show up. Upon entering, she'd said her last name was Moore and she now watched him with a suspicious, narrowed gaze as she shifted in her seat across the table from him and opened the file in front of her. The single overhead light hanging above them cast her ebony skin and dark eyes into harsh shadows and he had a crazy vision of her as a hawk and him as the prey.

He did his best not to fidget under her occasional piercing stares, when she deigned to look up from her paperwork. Heat prickled his skin beneath his frayed denim jacket and he longed to slide his finger beneath the stiff collar of his starched shirt and loosen his tie, but damn if he'd give Detective Moore the satisfaction of knowing how nervous he was. After all, he'd been here before and that time had turned out less than spectacular.

Finally, Detective Moore sat back in her chair and crossed her legs. "So, Mr. Evans. Why don't you tell me what happened? Perhaps we can cut a deal."

The last thing he wanted was to get on this woman's bad side, not when she was in charge of his case, but he wouldn't confess to something he hadn't done. Not again. He cleared his throat then swallowed hard. "I don't know what you're talking about."

"Don't be an idiot, Chase. We have your DNA on file. We can place you in the casino at the time of the murder. Possibly even in Warren Bryant's office."

Shit. He'd been careful when he'd went there earlier, but perhaps not careful enough. The police had obviously been there once already, considering almost everything in Bryant's office had been removed, but what if they'd gone back a second time? What if his crazy attraction to Bryant's daughter had made him reckless? He eyed Moore and kept his mouth shut.

And what if Moore was baiting him? He might've

dropped out of law school, but he still remembered the tricks of the trade.

Silent seconds ticked by like centuries. In the distance he heard muffled conversations and the smell of fresh brewed coffee drifted through the air. Moore scooted her seat back and stood, the scrape of metal screeching against the linoleum floor. "Fine, Mr. Evans. If that's the way you want to play this, I'll just tell the District Attorney you aren't cooperating."

So much for not getting on her bad side.

He hung his head. "I was at the Lucky Ace on legitimate business. You can ask my boss."

She arched a speculative brow. "Sleeping with the client is a part of your legitimate business?"

Jaw tense, he struggled to keep his tone even. "I did not sleep with Katherine Bryant."

"Then why was your hair on her pillow? What about your belt? It was covered with fingerprints and trace skin cells from both of you."

Chase scrubbed his hands over his face, praying the Rockfords would have his back in more than word only. "Look, she came on to me, all right? But I didn't want any part of her. I got out of there as fast as I could. Ask Blake about that too, if you want."

"How do you explain the vaginal fluids on the sheets? Someone had sex in that bed."

Thinking about Katherine Bryant and her fluids damned near made him ill at this point, but his lawyerly instincts kicked in as well. No one cared more about proving his innocence than him. It was high time he started planning his defense. "It's her bed. She could have had intercourse with anyone. Did you find any of my semen? My DNA, other than my hair?" He met Moore's dark gaze direct. "No. You didn't. Because I *didn't* have sex with her."

The detective shrugged. "Maybe you were extra careful. Used a condom. Cleaned up well afterward."

"And left the sheets behind? I'm an ex-con, but I'm not stupid." He took a deep breath. "Trust me, I wouldn't go near that woman with a ten-foot pole."

"Trust you, huh?" Moore's tone remained as flat as her expression. "That's a pretty tall order coming from a man with your past." She stepped a bit closer to the table and leaned in slightly. "Let's talk about Bryant's murder. Quite a coincidence she came on to you right before her husband ends up dead, don't you think?"

"Coincidence? Yes. But that will never stand up in court."

"Right." She flipped open the folder again. "You were in law school weren't you? Before your incarceration."

Chase did his best not to cringe, but couldn't hide

his reaction. He glanced up and caught Moore watching him closely.

"It's just a coincidence too then, I suppose, that Warren Bryant happened to be killed with an overdose of the same unique brand of heroin you went to prison for selling, right?"

His blood froze and the room around him seemed to tilt on a wonky axis before thudding back into place. *The same brand of heroin? What the almighty hell?*

Had Katherine been planning this to frame him all along? How would that even be possible? There was no way she could have known Chase would be assigned as bodyguard ahead of time.

Moore sat again. "Listen. Here's what I think took place, Mr. Evans. I think Katherine Bryant told you she would leave her husband for you, but when it came time for her to do it, she got cold feet. Therefore, having you kill Warren seemed like the best solution to her problem."

Chase forced himself to remain calm despite the turmoil roiling inside him. "Yeah? And when exactly would this alleged affair have occurred, Detective Moore? I've been out of prison for less than a week. I might've been a ladies' man back in the day, but even Channing Tatum couldn't work that fast. Never mind the fact I just met the woman for the first time the other day."

"Hey, if it's the right person, sometimes it only takes once." She flashed a small, frigid smile. "Plus, one time is enough for her to offer you a cut of her substantial inheritance if you did the deed."

He sat back and shook his head. "Still an awful big leap for two people who'd never met before." Chase crossed his arms, feeling a smidge more hopeful now that the police were at least suspecting some involvement on Katherine's part. Still not ideal by any means, but perhaps he could find more evidence to connect her to the death of her husband. "And an awful big risk on her part. You know, trusting an ex-con and all. Besides, you left out the most important fact, Detective Moore."

"Yeah? What's that?"

"I didn't kill anyone."

"Hmm." She nodded, her expression stoic. "Where were you yesterday afternoon around three?"

"Is that the time of death?"

Moore blinked at him, unmoving.

"Blake Rockford's house. I'm living there temporarily until I find a place of my own."

"Right." She pulled a pen from the pocket of her

light gray blazer and jotted some notes in the file. "Anyone who can corroborate your whereabouts?"

Damn. He'd been alone the whole afternoon until Blake came home. "No. But you have that time-stamped video, you can see when I went into the Bryant's condo and when I left the Lucky Ace, and I'm sure it will prove I couldn't have killed Warren Bryant." Hadn't Bryant's daughter mentioned something about that. Funny, now the video that had gotten him into trouble might just be the thing that cleared him.

"How do you know that? Do you know when he was killed."

"No, but I know I didn't do it. I wasn't even in the casino for more than an hour." Hopefully it wasn't the same hour within which Bryant was killed.

"I see." Her tone indicated what she saw was his flimsy alibi and a metric ton of bullshit between where they were now with the case and the ultimate truth. She scribbled a few more things in the folder then stood. "All right, Mr. Evans. You are free to go, but do not leave the city limits. This is still an active investigation and you are still a person of interest in the case. We may need to bring you back in for additional questioning at a later time."

Chase gave a curt nod and waited until the door

closed behind her before slumping in his seat. They didn't have enough on him to arrest him, that was good. But they'd keep looking and what if they found some stupid thing that incriminated him even if he didn't do it? His record as an ex-con wasn't going to help him. Eyes closed, he dropped his head back and wondered if he'd ever be allowed to move beyond his past and have a shot at a decent future.

SHELBY SAT in an arm chair in the corner of her stepmother's condo a few hours later, wishing she were anywhere but there and feeling decidedly out of place. It was bad enough her dad had spent his last days tied to a woman who saw him as nothing more than a paycheck.

Now, she had to listen to Katherine's totally fake sobs and carrying on. God, what she wouldn't give to be back at her shelter, caring for her stray animals. At least they gave her unconditional love and affection. No one else in her life ever had, that was for damned sure.

Even Dad, much as she'd loved him, had strings attached to his love.

Dad. Her chest pinched with sorrow. *I miss you so much.*

"All right, let's get started." The two detectives stepped into the center of the spacious living room and glanced between Shelby and Katherine, who sat in the middle of the long, white-leather sectional sofa. The female officer, Detective Moore, seemed to be running the show while the other cop—Detective Troy Atkins, he'd said—hovered in the background. Both wore badges that proclaimed they worked for the Homicide Division. Shelby still shuddered at the reminder of her dad's murder.

"Miss Bryant," Detective Moore said. "We'll start with you. Can you tell me if you noticed your father acting any differently in the days before his death?"

Shelby flinched. Her dad dealt with rather unsavory figures on a daily basis, which meant what was normal for most people would've been unusual for Warren Bryant. Still, he hadn't acted out of character, not that she was aware of anyway. "No."

"Okay. What about enemies? Anyone you know of who might want to cause your father harm?"

Other than the entire criminal underbelly of Las Vegas? Shelby bit back the snarky response before it emerged. She'd never approved of her dad's nefarious dealings, but he'd always kept her safe and provided well for her. She owed him respect for that. "Other than the transactions I'm sure you found in his business records? No."

"Yes." Moore said, her voice monotone. "We are following up on some...*questionable* accounts on his hard drive that was taken into evidence. Now, about your father's will. You stood to inherit a substantial sum after his death."

Dad's will? Shelby's stomach lurched. "Y-yes, but I never wanted it. His attorney's made me sign that paperwork and promised me they'd speak to Dad about having it changed, but then—"

"Oh, please." Katherine scoffed from the sofa, making a show of dabbing her eyes with her hankie. "Don't lie to the officers, Shelby. You knew. You knew that my Warren was having the will changed later this week. He was writing you out of it. But you couldn't have that, could you?" She broke into a fresh round of tears. "It was on his calendar, his appointment with the attorney. He'd drafted up a new will and was going to show it to me that night, except he never got the chance."

Katherine dissolved into sobs once more and it took every ounce of Shelby's strength not to roll her eyes. Or punch her out. Moore stared at her stepmother with cool indifference while Detective Atkins gave Shelby a quick, amused glance. The guy was attractive, in a slick, cover model sort of way, but she'd always preferred men who looked a bit rougher, a more world-weary edge. Guys like…

Images of her unexpected meeting with Chase Evans earlier that day flooded her mind before she shoved them away. *Hell. No.* He was most definitely off-limits. For so many reasons she couldn't even list them all.

Moore interrupted Shelby's train of thought and Katherine's grief show with more questions. "Ms. Bryant, you said your husband was having the will changed. How so?"

"I don't know." Katherine twisted her hankie between her fingers. "Like I said, I never got to see it and now it's missing. But I can tell you he never approved of Shelby's lifestyle. Never. In fact, they argued about it numerous times. He felt the money and the casino would be safer in my hands. Shelby knew he was going to leave most of it to me now even though I begged him not to. All I wanted was his love, not his money. But I guess Shelby wasn't happy with the new arrangement and she…she…"

Outraged, Shelby pushed to her feet. "Wait a damned minute. What are you implying exactly? That I had something to do with Dad's death? Because

that's insane. I couldn't care less if he signed every-
thing over to the next person who walked into the
Lucky Ace. Money means nothing to me. Nothing. All
I cared about was Dad and now he's gone and I—I—I"

Her throat constricted, severing her speech as hot
tears stung her eyes. A comforting hand landed on her
shoulder and Shelby found Detective Atkins by her
side, his expression sympathetic. At least someone in
this room seemed decent and human.

"Don't care about money, huh?" Katherine stared
daggers at Shelby from her place on the sofa before
transferring her attention back to Detective Moore.
"Have you seen how this girl lives? One look at her
apartment and you'll know exactly why she wanted to
get her grubby little hands on her daddy's money."

Shelby pulled away from Atkins and stepped
closer to Katherine, rage pulsing off of her in waves. "I
live exactly how I want. By *my* terms, by *my* merit. No
one else's. Unlike some other people." Trembling with
fury, she pulled a business card from her back pocket
and handed it to Detective Moore. "Here. I can't deal
with this anymore. If you have more questions for me,
please stop by the shelter. The address is on the card. I
need to get back to work."

She ignored their stares as she rushed from the
room. Leaving now wouldn't help her case with the

police, but she couldn't stand to be in the same room with Katherine one second more. All she wanted was to bury herself in her work until the world righted itself again. The elevator dinged and she climbed aboard then jammed the button until the doors closed and the car descended. Too bad her world would never be right again, not now that Dad was dead.

Shelby squeezed her eyes shut and leaned heavily against the wall.

Katherine was responsible. She felt it deep in her bones.

And somehow, someway, she'd prove it.

No matter what she had to do, no matter how far she had to go, she'd get justice for her dad. No matter what the cost.

6

———

Chase rolled over and stared at the alarm clock. 4:30 a.m. He'd gone to bed early the night before, despite Blake wanting him to stay up and watch the UNLV tourney basketball game. Not because of how exhausted he was—sleep was a rare occurrence in his life these days—but because he knew Laura's newspaper article was supposed to publish today.

On edge, he showered and shaved quickly, then pulled on the brand new pair of khaki pants and dress shirt Blake had brought home for him the night before. He'd kept a tab in his head of how much he was going to owe the guy once he was back on his feet. In truth, he knew it was a debt he'd never be able to repay, but still, he was determined to try.

Dressed and eager, he jogged downstairs and started some coffee, then walked down the hall to the foyer and cracked open the door enough to grab the morning Chronicle from the porch. This early in the morning it was only about fifty degrees out even in Las Vegas. The late-autumn air felt cold and crisp and he shivered slightly before stepping back inside and locking the door.

Taking the paper back into the kitchen, he was careful not to make too much noise and wake up Blake. He quietly fixed a mug of caffeine then took a seat on one of the stools at the center island and opened the newspaper to the front page. Sure enough, there was the story. Except, instead of Laura's picture and byline by the article, there was some guy by the last name of Davis. Plus, the more he read, the clearer it became this was not the story Laura had hoped to write. This Davis guy must have gotten the assignment instead of her. Just another piece of bad luck for Chase.

This story twisted the facts and pointed the finger directly at Chase as Warren Bryant's murderer, not Katherine.

Crap.

He rubbed his eyes and stood.

Air. He needed fresh air and space to figure out his

next move after this shitty bombshell of an article hit the airwaves. Time for more damage control. Hell, he should have those words tattooed across his forehead these days, since that's all he'd really gotten done for the last five years. And even then it seemed he'd only ended up screwing himself in the process.

After going upstairs to grab his jacket and phone from the guest room Blake had given him to stay in, Chase headed back downstairs. He stopped at the closet in the foyer and scrounged around until he found a black baseball cap, which he pulled on to help his disguise, then exited into the pre-dawn gloom. He walked the short distance to the nearby bus stop and waited for the first morning shuttle of the day to take him to Fremont Street.

His first foray to Warren Bryant's office had been interrupted by Shelby. Now, he needed the place all to himself to do some serious digging. He knew the cops didn't have anything solid, otherwise he'd be in jail right now, but what if they found something? He couldn't depend on the timeline of the video proving he was nowhere near Warren's office when he died. He wasn't even sure *when* Warren had died and Katherine was sneaky, she could have planted something or tampered with the video.

He couldn't rely on news articles or surveillance

tapes to clear his name. He had to catch the real killer himself. A sharp pang of guilt shot through him as he thought of Warren Bryant dead in his office. If Chase had been doing his job, Bryant would still be alive. Finding his killer would be one way to ease the guilt. Not to mention that it would keep *him* from going to prison for it.

He couldn't take another stint in prison.

Minutes later he put his money in the bus meter then found a seat near the back, tugging his collar higher to avoid being recognized. Like the words weren't bad enough, that damned article had splashed his former mug shots all over the place too. Nothing like a bit of unwanted publicity to crap on his already shitty parade.

As he settled onto the hard plastic bench seat, his phone buzzed. He pulled it from his pocket and scowled at the message onscreen from Laura Rockford:

So sorry about the article.
Definitely NOT what I wrote.
Dog Turd Davis rides again.

Chase wasn't sure who Dog Turd Davis was, but if he was even remotely related to the asshole who'd written those lies in the paper this morning, then he couldn't agree more. He stowed his phone away and stared out the window at the passing scenery. God, he was such an idiot. He knew the rules. Had learned them the hard way. Never trust another to do what you should do for yourself.

The bus rumbled into downtown Las Vegas and soon stopped near the corner of Fremont Street and Tower. He ducked out the back door and tugged his hat lower. Tourists still swarmed the area, so he decided to use the side alley to enter the Lucky Ace rather than the front or back entrance he'd used the day before. Head down, he started down the darkened street, then stopped at the sound of voices ahead. Quickly hiding behind a nearby dumpster, Chase peeked around the side in time to see two figures near the side employee entrance beneath a lone street light. One of them handed the other what appeared to be a wad of cash.

Memories assailed him like machine gun fire. Another drug deal. His brother Shane taking the cash. Chase begging him to get clean, to go straight. The police raid on their shared apartment later that night and the cops finding Shane's huge stash of heroin. Shane being hauled to the station in handcuffs, caught with enough smack to put him away for years, especially with his prior record.

Cold sweat broke out across Chase's forehead and the back of his neck. He slumped against the brick wall behind him and desperately tried to catch his breath. He'd had no choice. He would've done anything to save his little brother, done anything to keep him safe. Hell, he'd been keeping Shane safe for their entire lives. Safe from their abusive mother, safe from the dangerous world his younger brother had gotten himself involved in, safe from whatever came at them.

Chase squeezed his eyes shut and clenched his fists at his sides.

Shane would never have survived in prison and Chase was bound to get less time with his clean record, so he'd lied. Told the cops the drugs were his. Confessed to everything. The police, desperate for a conviction, took it as a slam dunk. Chase had gotten five years, with good behavior. Sure, it had cost him his career, his life, his future. But he'd do it all the same way again, no regrets, no questions asked. No hesitation.

The past slowly faded and Chase blinked up into the starless sky above. A breeze stirred and he rolled his head to the side, spotted one of the figures over the top of the dumpster, a hundred yards or so away. The person stepped into the pool of light near the door and bile rose hot and thick in Chase's throat.

Shane.

He turned away and pressed his hand to his mouth to keep from retching.

No. Please, dear God, no. Don't let this be happening all over again. Don't let my sacrifice have been for nothing.

Chase slid down the wall until his butt hit the asphalt and he wrapped his arms around his knees, tucking himself into a tight ball. Head lowered and eyes closed, he wondered what the hell his efforts were for. What was the point in clearing his name if everything he'd done, if all the sacrifices he'd made for Shane had been worthless?

7

"I need this delivered." Blake plopped a file down on Chase's desk a few hours later, startling him from the funk he'd been stewing in all morning. In all honesty, if someone asked him how'd he'd gotten here to the office, he couldn't tell them. He'd been so shocked at seeing Shane again in that dark alley that his actions had clicked into auto-pilot ever since and he'd all but forgotten about searching for evidence of Bryant's real killer.

Shane. My baby brother. The guy he'd taken a life-altering hit for, was back to his same old tricks it seemed. The dull pain in his chest intensified. *No. Not Shane. Shane wouldn't do that to me.*

That little voice in the back of Chase's brain spoke

up reminding him how Shane hadn't been there to meet him when he'd gotten out of prison, had rarely visited him, hadn't even tried to contact him since he'd been out. But those thoughts were too painful and Chase shoved the voice back down. There had to be another reason Shane had been in that alleyway, had to be another reason for the exchange of cash. Maybe he was working for a delivery company. Maybe he had a friend who worked at the Lucky Ace who owed him money. Maybe...

"Hello?" Blake waved a hand in front of Chase's face. "Anybody in there?"

"What?" Chase shook his head to clear it and sat forward in his chair. "Yeah, I'm sorry. Just a little distracted this morning."

Blake narrowed his icy gaze. "Everything all right?"

"Sure. Sure. Everything's fine." He stared at the folder Blake had placed before him and did his best not to wince. The words sound false even to his own ears. "What do you need me to do?"

"Deliver those quotes for security camera hookup and video file storage on our servers to a potential new client. Think you can handle that?"

Chase bit back a snarky retort. He needed this job, dammit, and a smart mouth wouldn't help him keep it.

"Yeah, I can handle it." He flipped open the file and scanned the contents. "Not sure why you don't just e-mail these though. Wouldn't that be faster?"

"Do you work for me or not?" Blake leaned his hip against the side of Chase's desk, his arms crossed. "I want them delivered in person. This could be a good new account for us and deserves some personal atten-tion." He glanced at the teetering stacks of filing Olivia had placed on Chase's desk. "Unless you prefer a slow death by paper cut."

"No." Chase sighed. "I'll deliver them."

"Good." Blake straightened and rattled off direc-tions for Chase, which he jotted down. "I'd give you the keys to the company car, but you haven't renewed your driver's license yet, right?"

No. That was something else on Chase's Need-To-Do list. He shook his head.

"I've got a few hours free next week. If you want, I'll take you over to the DMV and we'll get you squared away, all right? Then you can start using one of the company vehicles until you get a ride of your own, okay?"

"Okay." He pulled on his jacket and grabbed the file. "Thanks, man. For everything."

Blake shrugged and headed back to his office. "No

problem. Consider it an investment in your employment future. You'll earn it working here, trust me."

Outside, Chase caught the next bus heading toward North Las Vegas and took another look at the proposal in the file. It appeared to be for an animal rescue center called Paws and Play. Cute name. He flipped to the next page and studied Blake's security plan. Numerous strategically placed cameras both in and outside the building, plus 24-7 surveillance by Rockford Security's top IT department.

He was no expert, but he'd learned a thing or two from some of the thieves in prison. The plan Blake had designed seemed solid and the price reasonable. Should be a quick in and out delivery on Chase's part.

The bus pulled up to his stop and he departed then stared at the modest cinder block building in front of him. A plain rectangular sign with a rainbow-colored paw print in each corner proclaimed Paws and Play Animal Rescue Center. He opened the front door and stepped into a tiny reception area. The floor was checkerboard linoleum, the reception desk square and boxy and crammed full of brochures and small items for sale. The air smelled of disinfectant and wet dog.

A young, college-aged girl sat behind the desk in a cotton-candy pink colored scrub top strewn with cartoon drawings of kittens and puppies. Her short dark hair was streaked with green and blue and held back on one side with a sparkly rhinestone barrette in the shape of a skull. The girl smiled and gazed at him with polite disinterest. Her name tag read Steph. "Can I help you?"

"Uh, yeah." Chase stepped up to the counter. "I'm here to see the owner. I'm from Rockford Security."

Steph hiked her chin toward two empty chairs along the wall and picked up the phone. "Have a seat. I'll let her know you're here."

"Thanks." He did as she requested, aware the receptionist continued to watch him.

"I like your tats," Steph said after she hung up. "Get them around here?"

"Yeah." One of the guys in his cell block had run an ink parlor before his tax fraud conviction. Not that he'd tell some stranger that. "I got 'em around here."

"Cool." Steph chewed her gum loudly and picked up her magazine again. "She'll be right out."

"Thanks." He looked closer at the area around him. The place was small and crammed full of stuff, but extremely tidy. The floor sparkled beneath his black boots and a cheerful poster of a little boy and his puppy took up half the space on the wall across from him. Through the open doorway behind the reception desk filtered various yips and meows and barks and screeches of the place's residents. He wondered how many animals the shelter took in.

Another door opened in the opposite corner of the room and out stepped a woman he presumed must be the owner. Her back was to him, but something about her hair—below the shoulder, blonde, curly—seemed awfully familiar. She turned, and his heart skipped a beat.

Her. The girl from the office. Warren Bryant's daughter. Shelby.

Son of a bitch.

She seemed to recognize him in the same moment. Her steps faltered and her eyes widened. "You? What are you doing here?"

He stood and noticed once more how her height was damned near perfect for him. The top of her head would fit right beneath his chin, perfect for cuddling. Chase shook his head, bemused. He was here for work, not to pick up a date. He held out the folder. "My boss at Rockford Security asked me to bring these over. They're the quotes for your new security system." He forced an awkward smile and did his best not to blow the job for Blake. "So, you own an animal shelter, huh?"

Frowning, she snatched the file from him. "I didn't ask him to go through all this trouble. I told him I don't really have money in the budget for security."

Suspicion flared inside Chase. He should've known Blake was up to something. The guy used to pull schemes like this all the time on their old part-time security jobs. Always trying to set Chase up on blind dates. Always trying to work an angle for his own purposes. Never mind those purposes were almost always for the best interest for everyone involved. The idea of being manipulated rubbed Chase the wrong way. He'd had enough of being under someone else's thumb to last him a lifetime.

He shifted his weight and shuffled his feet as she glanced up at him again.

"I'm sorry, Mr.?"

"Evans. Chase Evans." The fact she didn't remember him from the other day stung more than he cared to admit. He'd remembered her name, and most everything about her. But then the hint of wariness and attraction in her blue gaze told him she hadn't forgotten him completely. *Huh. Interesting.* Hard to get. If that was her game, he'd play along. "And you are?"

Her light brown brows drew together. "Shelby Bryant. Listen, I don't mean to be rude, but unless you want to adopt a pet or volunteer, I don't really have time to chat. I've got a ton of work to do."

The sound of a popping bubble to his left drew their attention.

Steph, who watched their interaction with interest, at least had the decency to look embarrassed. "Sorry."

"Can you please go back and check on the parrots?" Shelby asked her.

"Yep." Steph nodded, disappearing through the doorway behind the reception desk after flashing Chase a quick smile. "See you around."

"See ya," Once she'd gone, Chase turned back to Shelby. "You really own this place?"

"Is that so hard to believe?" Her posture stiffened. He'd apparently stepped in it somewhere, but wasn't quite sure where. "For your information, I built this shelter from the ground up without any help from anyone." Her azure blue eyes blazed with indignation and Chase swallowed hard. If he wasn't careful, a man could get lost in those beautiful depths and never want to come out. "Well, except for maybe the government grants for non-profits."

"I'm impressed." Grant writing took time and expertise, as did running a successful business. She appeared to be good at both. "And all without help from your father or his money."

She visibly bristled at his words. "I have never

taken a cent of Dad's money. Not then, not now, not ever. And there goes my motive for killing him."

The steel in her tone buckled under her last statement and his heart ached for her. Regardless of what the evidence showed, he knew deep down that her grief was real. She didn't kill her father. No way. Judging from the slight tremble in her movements and her pale complexion she looked hunted, haunted, damned close to her breaking point. It was a look he knew well. The same look he'd seen reflected in his mirror every day before they'd shipped him off to prison. His fingertips itched to touch her, to pull her into his arms and offer her comfort, hope, understanding. Except, given their current situation, such advances would probably only earn him a swift kick in the nuts for his trouble.

So instead, he shoved his hands in the pockets of his khakis and rocked back on his heels. "Would you have time to give me a quick tour? I'd love to see how everything operates and it might be important for security camera placement."

Shelby eyed him warily for several seconds and he worried she might refuse. Then she gave a slight nod. "Okay. But quick is the key word. I've got deliveries coming and an obedience class for the new adoptees later this afternoon."

"Whatever you have time for would be wonderful."

She tucked the folder under her arm then gestured for him to follow her behind the reception desk and through the doorway where Steph had disappeared moments before. "This way."

He trailed after her into what appeared to be a small zoo, filled with dogs and cats and rabbits and ferrets. Several guinea pigs chomped nervously on lettuce as they passed by and a pair of brightly colored Macaws screeched and whistled from the far corner of the large open space.

"How many animals do you have here?" he asked, stopping in front of a cage containing a small, white, scruffy dog. The mutt reminded him of Skipper, his childhood pet. Man, he'd loved that crazy canine.

"About two hundred at any given time." She reached her fingers through the bars of the cage and coaxed the dog over. "How's my Growly doing today?"

"Growly?" Chase snorted. "Nice."

Shelby smiled and his breath hitched at how beautiful she was. "He's been with me for a while now. It'll be hard when he gets adopted."

"I bet." He squatted down and scratched the dog through the cage. "Occupational hazard, huh?"

She set the folder on a cage behind her then cooed

and whispered to the dog before turning to face him. "What do you mean?"

"Getting too attached. Getting hurt."

"Yeah. Getting hurt sucks."

Chase stood, almost bumping in to her. This close, her warm, minty breath fluttered over his face and he could spot a faint line of freckles drifting over the bridge of her nose. She seemed so clean, so untouched, so far from all the sins of his past. A past he wanted so much to forget. Their eyes locked for a few beats, then he stepped back before he did something stupid.

SHELBY FELT IRRESISTIBLY DRAWN to Chase especially since he was standing so close. He stepped back and she shook off the feeling even though she couldn't seem to break eye contact. He was the last man on earth she should want. After all, he could have had something to do with her father's death!

The sound of a clearing throat caught their attention.

"Sorry, Miss Bryant." Steph hovered near a row of rabbit cages. "I just wondered if there was anything else you wanted me to check on back here. The parrots are fine."

"Uh." Shelby inhaled sharply and did her best to focus on her work and not the man staring at her with fire in his eyes. "N-no. That's all for now. Thanks, Steph."

"Sure thing." The girl hustled out of the room, her sneakers squeaking on the linoleum and a knowing smile on her young face.

Shelby sidled farther down the line of cages, putting more space between them. "Is there something else you wanted?"

"Well, I—" Henry, a large green iguana who'd been climbing on some nearby cages, took the opportunity to pounce on Chase's head. To his credit, Chase didn't scream or try to bat the creature away. He just froze, his gray eyes wide. "What's on me?"

Shelby chuckled. "Oh, that's Henry. I think he likes you."

"And Henry is?"

"An iguana."

"Right." Chase reached up a tentative hand and stroked his finger down Henry's tail, which was now swatting him on the side of the face. "Nice to meet you, Henry. Now, if I could just move you over to one of these cages so your little nails aren't digging holes into my head, I'll be all set."

He leaned over toward a nearby cage, but if his wince was any indication, Henry only dug his claws in deeper. Shelby choked back laughter and sympathy. "Sorry, Henry doesn't go until he's ready. Was there something you wanted to talk to me about?"

"About catching the real person behind your father's murder."

"You mean besides you?"

"Funny." He scrunched his nose as Henry readjusted himself and now dangled his tail directly down the center of Chase's handsome face. "No. I was thinking more along the lines of Katherine."

"Katherine, huh?" It was a sweet dream, but so far she'd found zilch to prove her wicked step-monster was responsible for the crime. "Well, unless you plan to confess that you acted on her behalf, I don't have any proof that she did it."

Chase sighed and swatted Henry's tail away from his nose. "If we work together, maybe we can find some proof, something to put her away instead of me again."

Her resolve against him crumbled slightly. Having an extra set of eyes and ears on the case *would* help and it wasn't like he lacked motivation. Shelby had never been arrested, never been to prison. Hell, she'd never even set foot inside a jail—if you didn't count the old Mob Museum near the art district. But she imagined it wasn't someplace one wanted to go once, let alone twice. Still, she couldn't acquiesce so quickly. "Why would I want to help you get away with murder?"

"Seriously?" He gave her an exasperated look, even though he'd been a great sport about Henry thus far. "You don't really think I did it, do you? Katherine set me up."

No. Honestly, deep down, she didn't think Chase had killed anyone. But Katherine?

With all those remarks her stepmother had made to the police earlier, about her dad changing the will and insinuating Shelby had something to do with it all? Dread pooled low in her abdomen, weighing her down. Yeah. After spending years with that witch of a woman, she knew Katherine would kill the Pope himself if she thought it might make her rich.

Given her incendiary remarks to the detectives, maybe Chase wasn't the only person she was setting up, either. Shelby picked up a kitten out of a nearby playpen and rounded the far corner of the cages, nearing Chase once more. The tiny cat chirped in her arms, eyeing the irresistible lure of Henry's twitching tail.

Chase cocked his head to the side, his expression confused. "Is that kitten...chirping?"

"Yep." Shelby handed him the kitten and reached over to remove Henry from his head then place the iguana back on the front of a nearby cage. "They do that when they hunt."

"Good to know." He stroked the kitten's soft fur and smiled. "So, what do you say? Want to team up?"

"I don't know." She crossed her arms, feeling way more vulnerable than she wanted. "How do I know I can trust you? You *were* in Katherine's bedroom and there's your sordid past and the drug dealing. Never mind the fact the dealing took place in my dad's casino."

He cursed under his breath. "I should've remembered that."

"Remember what?"

"Nothing." He held up the kitten he was holding and grinned into its little black and white face. "What would I need to do to adopt this little guy?"

"You need a steady address, for one thing. If you just got out of prison, that would be a problem, right?"

"He's not for me. I want to get a pet for the guy I'm staying with."

"Oh." She took the kitten from him. "Unfortunately, it doesn't work like that. We have to conduct interviews with any prospective owners, run checks, do site visits to make sure the home environment will be compatible."

"I see." He looked genuinely disappointed and she felt a pang of regret. Still, the rules were in place for a reason and most of these animals had been abandoned once already. She would never put them through that again. "And you won't help me prove it was Katherine?"

"I don't know." She stared at him over the top of the kitten's head. "I'll need to think about it."

"Fair enough." He ran his hands through his hair then brushed a few stray cat hairs off the front of his jacket before pulling out a pen from his pocket and snatching the folder from atop the cage where she'd set it earlier. He scribbled something on the bottom of the estimate then handed it back to her. "Well, now you know where to find me once you decide."

Shelby followed him back out into the reception area then watched as he walked to the nearby bus stop to wait for the next shuttle. Much as she hated to admit it, the idea of teaming up with Chase Evans grew more appealing by the second. He seemed smart and strong and steadfast to a fault. In fact, the more time she spent with him, the more he seemed to defy all of her preconceived notions of what an ex-con would be like.

She watched as he helped an elderly lady off the bus and over to a bench before boarding himself.

Nope. Chase Evans wasn't what she'd expected.

Not at all.

8

Instead of going back to Rockford Securities, Chase caught a bus in the opposite direction and headed to an address he'd found on the Internet the night before.

He'd stayed up late last night searching public records sites for his brother's last known address and had been surprised to find he'd moved from the somewhat crappy Northeast Las Vegas apartment they'd shared together before Chase's incarceration to a more upscale community in a cushy complex downtown. He'd tried to keep tabs on his little bro while he'd been behind bars, but information was hard to come by and even then it was mainly second-hand. On the rare occasions when Shane had visited him—all two times during his time in prison—he'd never mentioned where he was living or what he was doing to earn his money. Now, Chase knew why. Too bad he hadn't known then that Shane's newfound prosperity had come from him falling back into his same old ways.

Crap.

Chase clenched his jaw and squinted out at the downtown landscape. The bright midday sun seemed to mock him from above. He wasn't sure yet exactly how he'd respond to seeing his brother again, especially after what he'd witnessed in the alley that morning, but whatever actions he took sure as hell wouldn't be all glittering light and rainbows.

The bus swerved to a stop near the corner and Chase stepped out onto the curb, a doorman in blue keeping watch over the apartment complex's entrance. Yeah, Shane had certainly moved up in the world these past five years, on the back of Chase's sacrifice and his damned drug money. Anger and betrayal seared his gut like molten lava. All those years, all those sacrifices, for what?

Chase inhaled sharply and forced himself to relax, flashing his most polite smile to the doorman.

"Can I help you, sir?" the doorman asked.

"Hi, um, yeah. I'm here to see my brother, Shane Evans."

"Is Mr. Evans expecting you?"

Thinking fast, Chase came up with an excuse. "Not exactly. I just flew into town this morning and I've got a couple hours layover. Thought I'd stop by and surprise him."

The doorman looked Chase up and down, taking in his Rockford Security ID badge, then gave a curt nod. "No denying the two of you are related, that's for sure. I don't normally do this, but I'll make an exception this time. I've got a good friend who works for Rockford Security. Great company."

"Yeah, it is." Chase shoved his hands in his pockets and said a silent prayer of thanks once more for Blake's trust in him. The guy had just saved his butt yet again. "Thanks, man."

"Have a great day, sir." The doorman let Chase inside.

He strode across the glitzy marble lobby and over to the elevators where he scanned the resident board for Shane's place.

Evans, S. Apt. 409

The ride upstairs passed in a flash, yet seemed to drag on forever and by the time the elevator dinged loud to announce his arrival on the fourth floor, Chase felt ready to burst, Hulk-style, from rage and determination. He walked the few steps to Shane's door and pounded twice, all thoughts of Shelby and whether or not she'd accept his offer shoved to the back of his mind. Now, it was all about Shane and Chase and some serious payback.

Seconds ticked by in silence. Chase raised his fist again, ready to bust clear through the goddamned door if no one answered. Then the sound of a lock clicking was followed by the door creaking open a tad to reveal his younger brother—bleary-eyed and groggy. Without waiting, Chase shoved the door open wider, causing Shane to take a step back.

Shane raked a hand through his dark, sleep-tousled hair, his low-slung boxers hanging off his thin hips and a large coffee stain in the center of his white tank top. Chase gave him a disgusted look and shook his head. Still a slob, even after all these years. He squinted at Chase with a lit cigarette hanging from his bottom lip. "What the hell, man?"

"What the hell is right!" Chase lost it, shoving his brother back then slamming the door behind him. "Mind telling me why you're still dealing? Why I rotted my ass in prison for five years for nothing?"

"Jesus, dude." Shane took a drag off his cigarette then exhaled slowly. "It's too early for this shit."

"It's noon."

"Seriously?" Shane scowled and leaned over to peer out the blinds behind him. "Fuck. I gotta get dressed, man."

"No." Chase stepped in front of him when he tried to pass, blocking his way. "What you gotta do is explain yourself. I took the rap for you, Shane. Lost years of my life all to give you a shot at making something of yourself, to learn from your mistakes."

Shane snorted, crushing out his cigarette in a nearby ashtray. Empty food containers and dirty clothes were strewn everywhere. The apartment would've been nice, if not for all the crap scattered around it. Well, that and the odor—a musty scent of dirty gym socks mingled with lavender air freshener. "Don't feel bad, bro. I did learn something. I learned never to keep the product in my house." He chuckled. "Won't make that mistake again."

A small muscle ticked near Chase's jaw, and he clenched his hands tight at his sides to keep from beating the living shit out of his brother. How could he have been so stupid, so blind not to see what a cocky, insufferable asshole his brother really was? The shy, scared kid he'd left behind had now morphed into an arrogant, unappreciative prick.

He turned away, too furious to speak, his throat

tight with adrenaline and hurt. From what he could see, the drug dealing biz must've been as lucrative as always. Several large leather chairs and a sofa filled the room along with a huge flat screen tv and a gaming console that would've made his buddies back in Cell Block G jealous. Hooks along one wall hung with designer outerwear that cost more than most people made in a month, fancy embroidered emblems covering the backs or the occasional front breast pocket. Built-in bookshelves lined the wall behind the entertainment center and the spaces were lined with dust-covered knickknacks and magazines and...

He narrowed his gaze on one particular pile of stuff. Stepped closer and brushed away the layer of grime to see shiny gold twinkling back. His commendations and awards from his security job days. Sadness and affection sliced through him. "You kept these?"

Shane sniffed then shrugged. "Yeah, so? Whatever. I thought they might be worth something, but they're not."

Chase turned back to the bookshelves. There was his certificate from the mayor and the engraved paperweight he'd received from the Chief of Police, but where was his letter opener? It had been covered in eighteen-carat gold and had been worth more than all the other ones combined.

I thought they might be worth something...

Realization ripped his fledgling forgiveness to shreds. Shane must've sold that one already. "What the hell happened to you, bro? You had so much promise. You could've gone to college, gotten a great life. You could've gotten out."

"Fuck you, man." Shane crossed his arms and glared with haunted gray eyes so similar to the ones Chase saw reflected back at him in the mirror each morning. "You don't know anything about me anymore. And I've done just fine without you. Not like I need life advice from a ex-con anyway."

Pain rendered him speechless. Chase blinked at the man he'd once given up his life for, his future for, and wondered how in the hell things had gotten so far off track from what he'd planned. He'd gone to prison so his brother wouldn't have to, gone to prison to give him the second-chance Chase had never had, would never have now if he didn't find something to clear his name again.

Shit.

From the belligerent look on Shane's face and his dickhead attitude, there wasn't much point in arguing.

"Jesus Christ." It was all Chase could think to say.

Resigned to the fact things with his brother wouldn't be getting better any time soon, he gave him one last look, then turned and left the apartment, still seething from Shane's shitty statements and his own inability to refute them.

AN HOUR LATER, Chase walked back into the Rockford Security offices, still pissed but back under control. The bus ride had helped. So had the walk around the block he'd taken before coming back in here again. It had given him time to think, time to assess what had happened so far and figure out where he wanted to go from here.

Good thing too, because he now had a bone to pick with his boss.

Chase made a beeline through the office and stopped at Blake's doorway. "Seriously. I just get out of jail and you're trying to set me up?"

Blake never looked up from his paperwork. "Hello to you, too."

"And not just set me up, but with the daughter of the man everyone thinks I killed, including her." He did his best to ignore that his outburst seemed to have drawn the attention of more than a few of his coworkers and lowered his voice slightly. "That's pretty damned twisted, man."

After several moments, Blake exhaled and slowly looked up at Chase, his famous arctic stare—The Hurt —on full display. With one dark brow arched, Blake sat back in his black leather office chair and crossed his arms. "Are you done?"

The guy made him feel like a misbehaving school kid, but Chase refused to back down. "You do realize that Shelby Bryant hates my guts, right?"

"What exactly are you accusing me of?" Blake's tone remained as cool as his expression.

"I don't know." Chase shook his head, frowning. "You were trying to set me up. You're meddling in my life." He scraped his fingers through his hair. "You're a...a...a frigging matchmaker, or something."

Shit. Matchmaker sounded like a woman, which Blake most definitely was *not.* Being a lawyer—or almost lawyer—he should've been able to use his words better, but he was out of practice and what he said would have to stand.

"Really?" Blake said the word with the same level of snark as a teenaged girl's eye roll. "Listen, I know you feel like a special snowflake these days, but honestly, I couldn't care less about your love life."

"Yeah? What about that meeting we had right

before all that shit with Katherine Bryant went down, huh? I distinctly remember you had your panties in a wad about what happened. You said you were glad I hadn't 'ruined my chances' and mentioned something about 'setting me up right' or something." He used air quotes for emphasis. "I thought you meant with the right job, but the choice of words was strange. And now you sent me over to Shelby's animal rescue with some trumped up quote on video surveillance she can't afford. Are you trying to fix me up with Shelby Bryant? Was this your master plan the whole time?"

God, now I just sound ridiculous.

A guy like Blake Rockford had far more important things to worry about than whether some freshly sprung felon could get a date or not. Much as Chase hated to admit it, he had been acting like some kind of prima donna since he'd gotten out of prison. Hell, he was damned near as self-absorbed as Shane these days.

"Look, Chase." Blake sat forward and rested his forearms on the desk, his hands clasped. "I hired you because you needed a job and because I know you're a good, *honest* worker. That's all."

The fact Blake confirmed his belief in Chase, and even inferred he knew about his wrongful conviction, made him feel like even more of an ass. Before he could say anything though, Blake continued.

"Now, are we done here? Because we both need to get back to work."

Chase let out his pent-up breath. "Fine. Yeah. I'm sorry about this, I just..." He shook his head and stared at his toes. "Just please don't send me on any more imaginary jobs trying to set me up with Shelby or anyone else, okay?"

"For the last time, I never tried to 'set you up' with anyone romantically, all right? But I do still have contacts at the police department and certain insights into this murder case and let me just say from what I've heard it would be beneficial to both you and Shelby if you guys called a truce and compared notes."

Stunned, he met Blake's gaze once more. "What do you mean?"

"I mean that when two people work toward a common goal, they have more success."

"So that side trip to Paws and Play wasn't about trying to get me a date?"

"Not unless you want one." Blake wrinkled his nose. "Though, I'd think you have more important things to think about right now. You know, like not getting accused of murder."

"Right." Chase turned toward the door. "Okay.

Thanks." He made it out into the hall again before Blake stopped him.

"And Chase?"

"Yeah?"

"Don't call me a matchmaker again. That's a job for little old ladies."

"Right. Sure thing, boss." Head down to cover the heat prickling his cheeks, Chase headed back to his desk in the corner. Even from across the room, he could see several new stacks of filing awaiting him. *Oh, goodie.* Unfortunately, he found his way soon blocked by several other members of the Rockford clan who herded him back toward Blake's door.

"Not a matchmaker, huh?" Logan Rockford, one of Blake's younger brothers and the company's Chief Financial Officer, said. "How about you assigning Dino to be Jan Winters' bodyguard? That seemed pretty matchmaker-y to me."

Logan flashed his older brother a devilish grin to which Blake gave him a flinty stare. "Dino was up in the rotation. That was all coincidence."

Garrett Rockford—yet another of Blake's younger siblings and the company's VP of sales—shouldered his way into the doorway beside Chase next. "C'mon. Like you didn't know they were high school sweethearts. You guys hung out at the house like every single weekend back in the day."

"And don't forget Laura and Mike." This from Olivia Rockford, Blake's younger sister and Chase's new direct supervisor. As Rockford Security's Chief of Operations, she kept the office running smoothly—and the stacks on Chase's desk growing ever higher. Together, the three Rockford siblings had effectively caged Chase in between them with no hope for escape. "You brought them together too."

She looked over at Chase and winked, her green eyes sparkling with barely suppressed mirth. He was all for some fun family ribbing, but not when it would irk his boss and potentially get him in trouble. He tried to ease out of their huddle once more, but to no avail.

Blake pushed to his feet and leaned over the desk, his voice terse but his icy blue eyes warm with affection. "For the last time. I am not now, nor have I ever, used this business to help people's love lives. Now all of you better get back to work before I fire all of your lazy asses."

"Aw, that's so cute, bro." Olivia gave Blake a sweet smile. "Being all tough. But we're all shareholders. No firing allowed. We can stand here all day and chat if we want and there's nothing you can do about it." She glanced sideways at Chase and hiked her thumb in his direction. "Well, except for him."

"And that's my cue to leave." He ducked out of the group again and this time they let him go. Glad for some space to breathe again, Chase headed back to his desk and the overflowing paperwork awaiting him.

9

"C'mon, Snickerdoodle." Shelby clucked her tongue to encourage the large, shaggy dog to follow her. With the enormous plastic cone surrounding his head it made things more difficult, but eventually he bounded up the creaking metal staircase on the side of her slightly shabby brick apartment building. Twilight had finally fallen on what had been one hell of a long day.

"That's it, boy," she encouraged, climbing the rest of the way up to her second floor studio, a cat carrier clutched in each hand. Technically, she wasn't supposed to keep pets here according to her lease, but all three of these animals were special cases. Snickerdoodle's fur was just starting to regrow after his previous owners had neglected him to the point where a skin rash had made him gnaw off his own skin to stop the itching. The two cats, as yet unnamed, had been brought in earlier that day with upper respiratory infections requiring round the clock observation for at least a couple of days. It wasn't like she could leave them alone at the shelter. They'd all been through enough already.

She reached the upper landing and set one of the carriers down to fish in her pocket for her keys, flipping on the porch light in the process. A legal-sized yellow packing envelope sat propped against her door. *Huh.* Thinking she must've missed the mailman again, Shelby unlocked her door then tucked the envelope beneath her arm and headed inside with her temporary menagerie.

"Okay, guys." Propping the door open with her foot to allow the dog in first, Shelby trailed behind with the cat carriers and closed the door behind her with her butt. She set the carriers on the floor and dumped her purse on top of one of them, then bent to open the cages. Both cats scrambled out and headed immediately beneath her overstuffed sofa.

"Perfect." She hung her head and figured she could coax them out later for their next round of medication, then turned to Snickerdoodle. "What about you, boy? You hungry?"

The dog padded over, tail wagging a thousand miles a second.

"Of course you are." She ruffled the fur behind his ears and straightened. "Typical guy. Well, let's get you something to eat."

The envelope crinkled under her arm and she laid it on the counter while she fixed Snickerdoodle a bowl of soft food. After she'd filled another with water and set it on the floor for him beside the food, she picked up the packing envelope again and scanned the outside. No postmark. *Weird.* Her pulse sped faster as she realized it couldn't have come from the mailman.

On edge once more, Shelby toed off her sneakers then headed back into her small living room. She didn't spend a lot of time here at the apartment, with her busy schedule at the shelter, but when she was home she liked the place to be cozy. She sank into an oversized armchair upholstered in light mint green, same as the sofa, and tucked her feet beneath her. If the envelope wasn't from the post office, then who had delivered it?

An image of Chase Evans skittered through her mind like a nervous church mouse. He'd shown up once today unannounced, perhaps he'd done it again. Shelby wrinkled her nose. *Nah.* They'd just met and he knew nothing about her, most especially where she lived.

Shelby shook her head. Chase Evans was nothing but bad news where she was concerned. It was in her best interest never to see him again, even if he might be her best chance of putting Katherine away.

She flipped the envelope over. Nothing on the back either. Shrugging, she tore it open. Best way to find out what was in it was to look inside. She pulled out the papers – a draft of Dad's will. Not the draft she and Chase had found in her dad's office a few days earlier, but a different one, a new one. She quickly looked it over and found this one left most of her dad's estate to Katherine.

Shocked, she lowered the papers and stared at the ceiling. So her step-monster had told the cops the truth the other day? Apparently, her dad really had changed his will. Except that didn't make any sense. He wouldn't do something so important without telling his only daughter, would he?

The clock above the stove in her tiny open kitchen showed six-thirty p.m. Maybe she could still catch someone at the attorney's office. Shelby reached over and grabbed her cordless phone from the shabby-chic end table and dialed.

"Butler, Cavanaugh, and Yates. How may I help you?"

"Yes, this is Shelby Bryant. I need to speak with Mr. Cavanaugh about my dad's will please."

"One moment." The receptionist's voice sounded bland as beige. Several seconds passed before she returned to the line. "Hold, please. I'll connect you."

"Rex Cavanaugh," the attorney said moments later.

"Yes, Mr. Cavanaugh." Shelby swallowed hard. For some reason, talking to this guy always made her feel like a bashful child. "This is Shelby Bryant, Warren's daughter. I received a new copy of my dad's will today. Someone left it on my front porch in an unmarked envelope." She was rambling, she knew, but couldn't seem to stop herself. This guy could care less about her mail. "I wondered if I could ask you a couple of questions."

Tone brusque, the lawyer dashed her hopes for answers. "Ms. Bryant, you know I'm not at liberty to discuss a client's personal business. I'm sorry."

He ended the call and Shelby sat a moment staring at the receiver before hanging up. In the few dealings she'd had with Rex Cavanaugh, he'd always been very nice, not at all like he'd just been on the phone. You'd think she would have a right to know her father's legal business now. Unless there was some other reason Rex couldn't discuss it. Maybe the police had him on a gag order or maybe Katherine had gotten to him somehow.

Okay, then. So much for that route. She replaced the phone in its charger then scanned the papers again. Nothing handwritten, all typed, except for her dad's signature and the attorney's. Both of those looked legit as well. Why would someone leave this on her doorstep, knowing it would only upset her, though?

Snickerdoodle, apparently done with his meal, returned to her side and lay down near the bottom of Shelby's chair on the hardwood floor. Having the animals around, even temporarily, at least helped ease her loneliness and anxiety. She rubbed her bare toes across the dog's back and sighed. Then again, maybe upsetting her *was* the point of the delivery.

And there was only one person who would get sick pleasure from that.

Katherine.

Shelby refused to believe her dad would change his will and leave everything to that money grubbing viper, especially without telling her. They were close, despite what Katherine told the police. Her dad loved her, even if he didn't always say it. And he sure as hell didn't trust Katherine, hence the prenup.

Dammit.

Shelby shoved the documents back in the envelope then leaned her head back against the chair. Katherine must've made the whole thing up to frame her. Eyes closed, she went over the earlier interview with the detectives once more in her mind. If Dad had changed his will, as Katherine wanted the police to believe, then that would create motive for Shelby to kill him.

What if Katherine had made the will up and sent it on purpose, so the police would find it in her possession? It wouldn't matter if it wasn't officially filed with the lawyer, Katherine could just claim it was her dad's draft, that he intended to file it. She'd even mentioned he had an appointment with the lawyer. And if the police found her with this, it would prove she knew her father was going to change his will—even if it wasn't true.

Plus, murder and the subsequent incarceration would most likely fall under the "Otherwise unable to inherit" clause her father had put in his real will. If Shelby was charged and sentenced to prison, she was pretty certain she'd lose whatever stake she had left in her dad's estate. And that meant that Katherine would get it all.

Shelby hadn't realized how devious Katherine was.

This fake will gave Katherine motive to kill Warren, too. But, she'd set the plans in motion brilliantly. Claiming that she knew Warren was changing the will and then killing him—or having him killed—before he had a chance to make it official was a stroke of genius. If the police bought her story, then they would think that Katherine would be the *last* person to want Warren Bryant dead before he could change the will to name her as beneficiary.

Katherine must have been planning this for a while. Which made Shelby wonder what else her evil step-mother had been planning.

You don't really think I did it, do you? Katherine set me up...

Chase's words from earlier returned to her mind. Given everything that had happened since her dad's death, she was becoming more and more certain that Chase Evans *was* telling the truth. She inhaled deep and opened her eyes to find Snickerdoodle now resting his head on her knee, his soft brown gaze staring back at her accompanied by a goofy doggy grin. Hell, maybe Katherine was trying to set up Chase too. Perhaps hedge her bets to throw the cops off.

"What do you think, boy?" She leaned forward and stroked her fingers through the dog's soft brown fur then kissed him on the snout. "Maybe Chase was telling us the truth all along, huh?"

As if in response, Snickerdoodle gave a low, short bark.

So, what do you say? Want to team up?

She stood and walked over to grab her purse off the top of the cat carrier then dig inside for the estimate Chase had dropped off earlier at the shelter. With her current circumstances, perhaps having some extra security around the place wasn't such a bad idea. That way, if anyone tried one of these anonymous drop-offs there, she'd catch them red-handed.

Near the bottom of the front page, his scribbled words shined boldly back at her: *If interested, call Chase Evans.* His cell number was below in blocky numbers.

Karma. That's what it was. The universe giving her the chance to apologize. Besides, both the kitten and Henry the iguana had taken to Chase right away today at the shelter. If that wasn't a sign he was a good person deep down, she didn't know what was. Animals were never wrong.

Smiling, she pulled out her cell phone and returned to her seat, tucking her toes beneath Snickerdoodle's warm tummy while he snored loudly. Yep, what went around came around, in her experience. And if she apologized to Chase for all her false accusations then maybe, just maybe, he'd still let her take him up on his offer to team up to find her dad's real killer.

———

TWO HOURS LATER, Chase stood in front of a plain white door of a somewhat rundown apartment complex not far from where he and his brother had lived before Chase's conviction in North Las Vegas. The area wasn't super bad and the cost of living was affordable, though he had to admit a bit of shock when he'd learned this was where Shelby Bryant lived. Even more shocking was her inviting him over to discuss a possible partnership.

Taking a deep breath and swallowing around the lump of tension in his throat, he knocked twice. A dog barked loud inside the apartment and Chase took a step back. Made sense for a single gal to have protection around here and the last thing he needed these days was to get mauled. Plus, given what she did for a living, he should've expected at least a few critters sharing her living quarters.

The door cracked open and Shelby peeked out. "Hey."

"Hey." He rocked back on his heels, unsure what

else to say. Not that he had to worry. Before he could utter another word, a huge, fluffy ball of fur charged out the door and tackled him back against the railing of the second-floor landing. Dog breath and slobber covered his face as the mutt's large plastic cone blocked out Chase's world.

"Sorry about that," she said, grabbing the dog by his collar and pulling him back inside the apartment. "Are you okay?"

"Yeah." He ran a hand over his face and chuckled. "Friendly pooch, huh?"

"Not usually, no." Shelby stepped aside to allow Chase in, then closed the door behind him. "Snickerdoodle doesn't usually like strangers. Especially men. He was neglected and his past is kind of sketchy."

Chase crouched to pet the dog properly. "Guess we have something in common then don't we, boy?"

Shelby gave him an odd look then stepped into a small, galley-style kitchen that was open on one side to the living room. The place was neat and cozy, if tiny as hell.

"Must be hard keeping a big dog like this in such a small apartment." Chase laughed as Snickerdoodle pressed his plastic cone against Chase's chest and snuffled. "How long does he have to wear this thing?"

"He's fine. I take him for lots of walks down at Bell

Park. And hopefully, he'll only need the cone of shame for a few more days. His fur's coming back in pretty nicely now." She opened the fridge then looked at him over her shoulder. "Can I get you something to drink?"

"No. Thanks." Chase ran his hands down the dog's somewhat gaunt sides and noticed the bare patches of skin on his haunches. "Bell Park. That brings back memories. Used to play there when I was a kid, then hung out there as a teenager."

"You used to live around here?"

"Yeah." Chase stood and wiped his hands on the thighs of his jeans. "So, you want to team up, huh?"

She opened a bottle of water and took a large gulp before answering. "I think Katherine's trying to frame me for my dad's murder. I figure we've both got reason to prove our innocence. So, let's find out who the real killer is. If it's Katherine, great. If not..." She shrugged.

"I think we both know it's her." He crossed his arms. "Who else could it be?'

"I don't know." She frowned. "But I'm trying to keep an open mind. Katherine's crafty though. If she did do it, anything could be a clue."

They settled on the overstuffed sofa in her living room—each on opposite ends—to concoct a plan of action.

Chase took off his denim jacket and draped it over

the back of a nearby chair and decided to address the elephant in the room first. Walking on eggshells wasn't his specialty. Not anymore. "Listen, before we get started, you understand if we work together we'll need to get along. And you'll have to trust me."

"That works both ways." She watched him over the rim of her bottle. "I'm game if you are."

"Good. Fine. Okay." He scooted back into the corner of the sofa. "What have you done so far?"

"Other than checking my dad's office the other day? Nothing. But I think Katherine has a plan. She sent me a fake will."

"Fake will?"

"Yeah. Check this out." Shelby grabbed an envelope from the kitchen counter and handed it to him. The simple will inside looked official, but why would it be sent to Shelby all of a sudden like this?

"This says your father was leaving everything to Katherine, but it's a draft. It's not official yet."

"Yeah, but I called the lawyer. They wouldn't tell me anything but I know my father wouldn't do this. If he was going to change things he'd talk to me first. The will that was in his safe is the real will."

"And you think Katherine had this made and sent it to you? Why?"

"Who knows? To get me all riled up, probably. She probably thinks it will make me do something stupid."

"Or that it would be a motive for you to kill your father, to prevent it from being recorded officially."

"WHICH MEANS we better find something that proves she's the killer fast before she does something else."

"Hmm." Chase crossed his arms. "Blake told me the other night your father had secret security cameras installed in his office. Feeds he didn't share with anyone. Blake said he'd tried to talk him out of it, in case of a break in, but Warren wouldn't budge."

"I believe it." Shelby snorted. "My dad's line of work had him dealing with less than savory characters sometimes. I didn't approve and was worried about him, but he always told me he had it under control."

"Right." Intrigued, Chase wanted to know more, but her troubled expression told him not to push. Not yet. They'd be spending a lot of time together over the days ahead. There'd be time for asking those questions later. "Well, if we can access those feeds, there's a good chance the real murderer is on them. Any idea where they might be?"

"Nope. We should probably check Katherine's

condo too. And the Rockford Security feeds. Maybe we can find something there."

"I can handle getting us access to the Rockford feeds, no problem. Katherine's condo though." He scrunched his nose. "I'd be thrilled if I never set eyes on that place again."

"Too bad." Shelby grinned and nudged him with her foot. "We're a team, remember? Fifty-fifty or it's a no-go."

Chase sighed. "Fine. But I won't like it."

"Neither will I, trust me."

"I do." He smiled at her, realizing for the first time in a long time, it was true. He hadn't trusted very many people since going to jail, but he trusted Shelby. "I'll ask Blake for access to the footage from the casino floor too. There could be something the cops missed on there. We can probably look at them tomorrow, if he's okay with it."

"Great. What time should I meet you in the morning?" She straightened and set her water on a nearby coffee table. "And where are the offices again?"

"If you're busy at the shelter, you don't have to be there."

"Like hell I don't. You're not going to do this alone. If we're in this together, I'm going with you. Besides, two sets of eyes are better than one, right?"

"Right." He rattled off the address for Rockford Security. "It'll need to be early, say around seven, since IT will get swamped later with the regular daily feeds."

"No problem. Seven works great for me, actually. I can go there before I hit the shelter for the day."

A series of meows issued from beneath the sofa, followed by two cats emerging then jumping up on Chase's lap. One was smoky gray and his angry face would've given Grumpy Cat a run for his money. The other was an orange and white tabby. Both snuggled up to Chase's sides like he was their favorite cardboard box. Frowning, he held his arms up and stared down at the newly purring creatures. "Uh..."

Shelby laughed. "You do have a way with animals, don't you?"

"Apparently."

She reached over and picked up the tabby, putting it on her lap and stroking its head. "So, I guess we have a plan."

"Yep." Chase tried to lower his arm and received a warning hiss from Cranky Kitty. "Hey, I've been thinking a lot about those animals earlier at the shelter. I still think I'd like to adopt one for my boss, if that's okay."

"Like I said, we have procedures to go through,

but…" Shelby kissed the tabby's nose then smiled at Chase. "I guess I could make an exception for you since your boss is well known. I'm sure he'll be a good parent to his new pet."

"Good."

"I can stop by the shelter and bring the kitten with me in the morning, if you want."

"Oh." Chase placed his raised hand behind his head. "Um, actually I was thinking of the other one now. The iguana?"

"Henry, you mean?"

"Yeah. Henry."

"Sure." Shelby stood and Chase followed suit. "I've been trying to place him for months, so this is good. I'll bring him with me tomorrow. What made you change your mind?"

Chase tugged on his jacket and headed for the door. "He seems sort of broody and opinionated, kind of like my boss. Not to mention that head jumping trick." Chase snickered. "Blake'll love that."

10

Shelby stood outside the Rockford Security offices bright and early the next morning. *Okay*. Maybe more on the early side than bright, but still. She clutched Henry's leash tighter in her hand as a group of tourists passed by and snapped photos of the crazy lady with the iguana on her shoulder.

Henry didn't seem at all fazed by the attention, his tiny claws clutched tight to the soft cotton of her pink T-shirt, and his tongue flicking out occasionally to tickle her ear. Shelby sighed and glanced sideways at him. "Where is Chase, huh?"

She checked her watch again and shifted weight from one foot to the other. Technically, she was still a few minutes early. Maybe he'd already gone inside without her. Standing out in the open like this made her feel too vulnerable. Made her feel like Katherine might be watching her with a pair of binoculars, searching for more ways to screw up her life.

As if on cue, a bus swerved to the curb near the corner, exhaust belching as the doors screeched open and several passengers exited. One man was particularly noteworthy. Tall, muscles for days, dark hair, and stormy gray eyes. She swallowed hard as Chase waved and headed in her direction.

No wonder Katherine had tried to seduce him.

Tried, but not succeeded. Shelby was convinced Chase was telling the truth about that. Chase had been with Katherine the night her father died, but he hadn't been in the condo long enough for much to happen. She'd checked with the driver and then compared that to the time on the surveillance tape that showed Chase running out.

Her stomach lurched at the idea of Chase and Katherine—or any woman for that matter—together and unexpected envy pinched her heart. Shelby inhaled sharply and scowled. What was up with that? It wasn't like she wanted him for herself.

"Hey," Chase said, coming up beside her. "I see you brought our friend."

"Yep." Her tone sounded overly chipper, but she didn't care. She passed him Henry's leash and their fingers brushed. He met her gaze and she saw a tiny flicker of emotion there before she looked away fast. The iguana jumped to Chase's shoulder and she hurried inside suddenly feeling awkward. "We should get upstairs."

"Sure." He followed behind her, his expression amused as he cooed to the lizard now cuddled up to the side of his neck. They caught the elevator and took the short ride to the fifth floor where Chase said the IT offices were located. "How are you feeling this morning?"

Shelby gave him some side eye before answering. "Are you asking me or Henry?"

Chase chuckled. "Both."

"I'm good, thanks. And Henry's his usual charming self."

"Awesome." The doors dinged open and he escorted her to the IT front desk. A short guy with a messy flop of brown hair approached them.

"Hi, can I help you?" the guy asked. His name tag read Brandon.

"Hey, man." Chase gave the guy a friendly hand-shake. "Blake sent us to see some security footage."

"Oh, right. What time is it?" Brandon rubbed his eyes.

"Seven a.m.," Shelby answered, smiling.

"You're kidding."

"Nope." Chase pointed at the nearby wall clock. "Says so right there."

Brandon held out his hand to Shelby. "Brandon Sterling."

"Shelby Bryant."

He winced slightly, pink coloring his cheek. "Oh, right. Sorry to hear about your father."

"Thanks."

He escorted them back to his cubicle and took a seat behind his computer, typing in a few commands before stretching his arms above his head. "Should take just a second for the feeds to load." He looked over at Shelby, his dark gaze narrowed. "Shouldn't you be with one of the VIPs rather than this guy?" He looked at Chase then back to her again. "Not that Chase here isn't a good guy, and I can see him not wanting one of the Rockfords to steal you away, but—"

Chase stepped closer to the guy's chair, hands clenched. "Just bring up the footage, please. Blake said we could look at everything—the casino floor, the lobby and hallway, Bryant's office."

Confused, Shelby glanced at Chase. Her dad did indeed have special cameras in his office, she doubted he'd store the feeds on the Rockford servers. Then again, Chase might've found out something new and hadn't had a chance to tell her yet.

Brandon, however, cut that dream short. "Nope. None of our cameras were in the big guy's office."

"Damn. Okay." Chase caught Shelby's eye and winked conspiratorially. "Just show us what you do have then."

"Grab another chair and pull it over, man." Brandon stood and gestured for Shelby to take his seat then pointed to an empty cubicle across from his. "This could take a while for you guys and I'm heading home."

Shelby sank into his chair, nervous flutters filling her gut. "You're not staying?"

Being alone with Chase shouldn't bother her. It wasn't like she was afraid of him, she just suddenly felt sort of awkward. Oh well, at least Henry would be there.

Chase wheeled another chair over and took a seat to the side and slightly behind her, his warmth both comforting and disturbing as hell. "So what do we push?"

"This key is Play. This one is Fast Forward, this one Reverse." Brandon pointed to the keyboard in front of Shelby. "And this one here is Pause." He grabbed his jacket from a hook on the cubicle wall then backed away slowly. "All right kids. Try not to have too much fun without me."

Once he'd gone, Shelby glanced over her shoulder at Chase. They stared at each other for a moment while Henry scampered down from Chase's shoulder and made himself at home on top of the nearby computer tower, apparently basking in the heat it generated.

"We, uh, should probably get started." Chase leaned in closer and hit Play.

"Yeah." Shelby swallowed hard and did her best to concentrate on the video on the screen. The time stamp in the corner of the feed showed the day of her dad's murder and soon Chase's infamous exit from the elevator appeared on screen, followed by several minutes of nothing, until they fast-forwarded through to when the police arrived on the scene.

"Let's switch to the condo footage instead." Chase pointed to one of the other keys. Shelby clicked it, then flinched when Katherine's face popped up. She resisted the urge to squirm in her chair—now she'd see what had really happened with Chase and Katherine.

Shelby concentrated on the computer monitor. Katherine walked into the living room of the condo with Chase trailing behind, loaded down with bags and boxes. Katherine pointed to a chaise lounge across the room then disappeared into the bedroom. A moment later, Chase followed. Within minutes, he bolted from the room again, fiddling with the fly of his pants.

As if sensing her surprise, Chase leaned in close and whispered. "I did *not* sleep with her."

"Of course not," she said, her tone snarky. She knew she was being bitchy, but was too rattled to care. Chase had denied anything happened, but clearly *something* must have in order for his pants to be undone. "You were just zipping up your pants for some other reason."

"She cornered me. I was trying to fend her off and still keep my job. By the time I got away, she'd taken off my belt and was working on my pants, but thankfully nothing else happened. Besides, you can see by the timestamp I was only in there a few minutes."

"And a few minutes isn't enough time for sex?"

Chase gave her a sly grin. "Not with me, baby."

Damn. She'd walked right into that one. Cheeks heated, she looked away fast.

After several awkward moments, Chase sighed. "Look, don't you think it's kind of weird that your father had a security camera in his living room, though?"

"Not really." Shelby crossed her arms. "He used to have meetings at the condo sometimes. Things he wanted to tape. You can turn it off pretty easily."

"Did Katherine know that?"

"Of course."

"Hmm." Chase frowned and rubbed his hand over his jaw. "And yet she didn't. Even when she was trying to get me into her bedroom."

"Yeah," Shelby said, swiveling toward him and picking up on his train of thought. "It's almost like she wanted to get caught or something."

They ran the tape back and watched it again. After his onscreen-self stormed out of the condo, Chase reached past her to stop the feed. Tense, he pointed toward a corner of the screen near the hallway where a shadow appeared, then vanished in the blink of an eye. "Did you see that?"

"Yeah, but it was awfully fast. It could have been anything."

"Like hell." He hit Rewind for a few seconds then replayed the end again. The shadow blipped on screen, then gone. Same as before. After that the feed went black, the camera off. "Shit."

"Let's keep looking." Shelby shooed his hands away and clicked on the next feed. "Maybe Katherine met with the killer some time earlier in the week."

"Fine with me. That gives me a rock solid alibi. Early in the week, I was still a resident of Cell Block G."

She clicked Play then sat back. This video showed Shelby and her dad. From their wild gestures and angry expressions, she and Dad were obviously fighting again. Most likely over money. She reached out to fast forward through it, sorrow constricting her chest.

Chase stopped her, taking her hand in his. "Wait. What's this?"

"Nothing. It was a stupid fight. We made up the next day."

"Well, that *nothing* was caught on tape, and it won't do you any good when the police get their hands on it."

Dread bubbled thick in her veins. He was right. This would play right into Katherine's hand. And speaking of Katherine, the feed looped back to her condo again, showing her stepmother trying to hide what appeared to be an envelope full of money in a drawer in one of the living room tables.

"What the hell?" Shelby glanced from the screen to Chase.

"Maybe we *do* need to check out Katherine's condo again."

"Maybe." She replayed that section of feed again, paying attention to exactly where her step-monster had stashed the evidence. "We'll need to wait until nightfall. Katherine only goes out during the day to shop or get her nails or hair done. But she always goes down to the casino at night, then sometimes out on the town. We can sneak in there while she's away."

Chase nodded, tilting his head toward the screen. "Anymore tapes? Wouldn't want to miss anything."

They watched about twenty more minutes before a gorgeous woman in a designer power suit interrupted them. Her green gaze darted from Chase to Shelby then back again, her smile sly. "Figured I'd find you here. Guess Blake's little scheme worked, eh?"

Crimson dotted Chase's high cheekbones.

"What scheme?" Shelby asked, confused. Unsure how to proceed, she introduced herself. "And, um, I'm Shelby. Shelby Bryant."

"Olivia Rockford." They shook hands. "And please call me Liv. Everyone does. I bet my brother is playing matchmaker again. He's trying to hook you guys up."

"Please," Chase said, his gray eyes wary. "It's not like that."

Shelby shook her head, disturbed at how ridiculously giddy the thought of being 'hooked up' with Chase made her feel. "Really. We're not 'hooked up'."

Liv tossed her long brown hair over her shoulder and narrowed her gaze. "What are you both doing here then?"

"Work." Chase pointed at the computer screen. "We're working."

Liv leaned in and squinted at the security feeds, then Chase. "That's not work. You've been pulled off of the Lucky Ace detail. I signed off on the paperwork myself. You know, as your new boss."

"I thought Blake was your boss."

"Blake thinks he's everybody's boss." Liv chuckled.

"Liv is my immediate supervisor."

"Yep. And the company decided it would be better if our boy here stayed as far away from Katherine Bryant as possible."

Shelby snorted. "I can see why."

"God! For the last time, I did *not* do anything with that woman!" Chase growled.

"Good thing too. Blake would've knocked you upside the head for that one. And is this a new friend of yours, Chase?" She reached over and ran a finger down the lizard's back. Henry scurried around on top of the computer tower to check out his new admirer. "Who's a good iguana, huh? Who is?"

"Thanks for your vote of unconfidence." Chase said, his tone irritated. "And his name is Henry."

"Henry, huh? Nice. And you're welcome." Liv patted Chase on the shoulder, completely ignoring his now churlish demeanor. "And any time you need a healthy dose of straight-up honesty, I'm your gal. Besides, I aim to please when it comes to my employees." She smiled at Shelby. "It's good you guys are 'working' together to solve this mystery. Did Chase offer you a tour of the place? Would you like to see the executive offices upstairs?"

"Um, okay. Sure." She stood and moved in beside Liv. "Is that okay with you, Chase?"

He didn't say a word, just gave a curt nod.

"Great." Shelby grabbed her purse. "And while I'm here, if I could possibly talk to Blake Rockford as well? He's going to install some security cameras at my animal shelter for me."

They started to walk away and Chase called out from behind them. "Don't worry. I'll just stay here and finish looking at all these tapes by myself."

Liv snaked her arm through Shelby's and tugged her forward to the exit when she hesitated. It didn't really seem fair to leave Chase behind to do all the work, but she did need to talk to Blake and Liv seemed really nice and...

They walked out into the outer hall again and headed toward the elevators. Liv pushed the Up button then grinned at Shelby. "So, have you kissed him yet?"

Heat prickled her cheeks and she wondered if it was too late to run back into IT with Chase. But the elevator dinged and Liv dragged her onboard. "What? No. And I'm not going to either. We have a strictly business relationship. Besides I don't really know him ..."

Liv jabbed the seventh floor button then leaned back against the shiny metal wall. "You don't believe that assertion about him and Katherine, do you?"

Shelby shrugged. "No, but ..."

"I don't believe it and neither does Blake. Same thing with his drug trafficking conviction. That whole thing was bullshit. I've never met any man more trust-worthy than Chase Evans."

Shelby eyed Liv from across the elevator, her thoughts churning. So, Blake and Liv thought Chase hadn't broken the law. Good to know for future refer-ence. Though, then why did he go to jail for five years? The Rockfords seemed to trust him though and that added another check in her imaginary "Reasons to Like Chase Evans" column.

AN HOUR LATER, Chase shut down Brandon's computer and stood to stretch. The next shift of IT guys had arrived and the place now buzzed with activity. Henry scrambled from the top of the computer tower to Chase's shoulder then they headed back to the elevators to find Shelby. Her tour with Liv should've been over by now. There wasn't that much around here to see.

He pushed the Up button and stepped back to wait, hands shoved in his pockets and Henry's leash dangling loose down the middle of his chest. Honestly, he'd had the green guy brought over as payback for all of Blake's nosiness and scheming, but the more time he spent around Henry, the more he liked him. It was nice to have someone around who didn't judge, didn't care about his past at all. Only cared about his body heat and the occasional tickle under his jowly green chin.

Chase looked to the side and performed said scratch now, chuckling as Henry's tongue snaked out to flicker over Chase's cheek.

"That's my little man," he cooed.

The elevator dinged and the doors opened. He stepped forward without looking and damned near collided with Shelby.

"Oh!" She put her hands on his chest to stop him from barreling over her. "Sorry."

"Jeez, no. I'm sorry." Chase halted and grabbed Henry's leash to keep him from toppling off onto the floor. A fresh wave of embarrassment crashed over him. As if Liv's teasing earlier hadn't been bad enough, now he looked like an impolite imbecile too. "I didn't see you there."

"No problem." Shelby removed her hands from him and moved sideways, increasing the space between them. "You were distracted." She glanced from him to Henry and back again. "He's pretty adorable, isn't he?"

"Yeah. He is." Chase grinned over at his newfound reptile bud, then shuffled his feet and stared at the toes of his black boots. "How was your tour?"

"Great, thanks. Blake wasn't in, but I spoke with Garrett about the cameras and then Liv showed me around. Nice place. Did you find anything else on the security footage?"

"Nah, not really," he said. "Katherine seemed to be on her cell a lot in the tapes. It looks like she has two phones. Maybe one is a burner phone that she uses for plotting and scheming. If we can find a way to get her phone records or make sure the police have them, that might help."

"Maybe."

The elevator dinged again. A group of computer guys got off and headed for the IT offices while Chase held the door for Shelby then stepped in behind her. He'd been headed to Blake's office to thank him for setting up the viewing of the security footage, but she'd said he wasn't in yet. So he pushed the button for the lobby instead and rode down with Shelby. "Are we still on for the Lucky Ace tonight?"

"Absolutely. Meet me in the staff parking lot around back at ten."

He wrinkled his nose. Technically, that was after his court-mandated curfew. Blake had somehow managed to convince the judge not to put him on house arrest and give him one of those oh-so-attractive ankle bracelets during his parole. Breaking curfew would just be this one time and for a good cause, but he hated taking the chance of jeopardizing Blake's hospitality and good faith in him. Good faith was a rare gem in his world these days.

"Is that a problem?" Shelby frowned when he didn't answer.

"No. No. It's fine." Chase shrugged off his concerns. If he and Shelby continued on their plan to find the real killer, breaking curfew would be the least of his problems. Besides, he had bigger fish to fry at the moment. "Hey, uh, I'm sorry about that whole matchmaker thing with Liv. Blake and I used to work security jobs together back before he joined the police force and I...well, before everything happened. Anyway, all the Rockfords kind of feel more comfortable around me because of that and treat me like one of the family. She's not normally quite so informal around people she's just met."

"It's fine." Shelby smiled, the look in her pretty blue eyes oddly amused. "She seems nice."

"Yeah, she is. Smart as hell too."

"Sounds like someone's got a crush?" Shelby's gaze narrowed.

"What?" Chase scoffed as Henry wrapped his tail around his neck. "Me? No. She's my boss, for Christ's sake. Why would you even say that?" He lifted his chin slightly, picking up on her teasing tone. "Why? Are you jealous?"

"Are you insane?" She snorted and shook her head. "You wish."

Yeah, I do.

"What if I did?" He stepped closer to her. Henry seemed to take the hint and climbed down his arm to perch on the waist-level railing running around the middle of the elevator. *Smart lizard.* Shelby's breath hitched and Chase got the impression that if he leaned over and kissed her, it would not be unwelcome, he was just debating whether or not to do it when...

Ding. Ding.

Chase cursed inwardly and leaned back, grabbing Henry's leash before he bolted out the now open doors in front of them.

"Well, well. Look who we have here."

Blake.

Chase glanced at Shelby, took in her flushed face and dreamy expression and knew he was busted. He held out his arm for Henry to climb then ran a somewhat shaky hand through his hair while the iguana settled in on his shoulder once more.

Blake held the doors open with one hand and extended the other toward Shelby, his smile wide and knowing. "Blake Rockford. You must be Shelby Bryant. So nice to finally meet you in person. Your father told me so much about you, I feel like I know you already."

"He did?" Shelby asked as she shook Blake's hand.

It damned near broke Chase's heart to hear the surprised hopefulness in her voice and see her tragic expression whenever someone mentioned her late father. It was obvious she idolized the man, but from her reactions, it didn't seem like those sentiments had been returned. Chase felt unexpected anger surge through him and the unaccountable need to beat the shit out of anyone who didn't treat Shelby with the respect and admiration and kindness she deserved.

"He did," Blake confirmed, ignoring the persistent buzz of the elevator alarm. "He was very proud of you."

"Oh." Her soft creamy cheeks turned a deeper shade of rose. "Well, thank you." She tucked a stray blond curl behind her ear and stepped forward to sidle past Blake. "I was just leaving."

Chase remained where he was while Blake stepped in beside him, praying to God that Shelby wouldn't utter the words he already knew she would.

She turned back and waved to him. "So, I'll see you tonight, Chase?"

Damn.

He didn't miss the side eye Blake gave him, or his boss's cocky half smile.

"Uh, yeah. See you later," he managed to say before the doors slid closed once more. Chase slumped into the corner of the elevator and did his best to distract himself from the weight of Blake's stare. Henry helped, by digging his sharp little claws into Chase's shoulder. Pain was good. Pain was real. Pain was what he was used to.

"Mind telling me about *that?*" Blake said, his tone amused.

"What?" He tried to play dumb. "You mean Shelby? I thought you said you didn't care about my love life."

"I don't." Blake snickered. "I was talking about the lizard."

"Oh, yeah." He cocked his head to the side. "This is Henry."

Chase passed the leash to Blake and Henry jumped from his shoulder to his new owner. A weird sense of loss filled him as he watched the iguana cuddle into Blake's neck like it was home. *That.* That's why it didn't pay to get close to anyone or anything. Couldn't trust them. Eventually, they always moved on and left you behind. He squared his shoulders. "Have fun. He's yours now."

"What?!" Blake's expression shifted from playful to concerned. "I don't think I'm ready for a pet."

"Yeah? Well, remember when you sent me down to Paws and Play even though I wasn't ready? Payback's a bitch, man. Shelby let me fill out the paperwork in your name. Enjoy!"

They arrived at the executive offices on the seventh floor and exited the elevator. Chase headed down the hall ahead of Blake, calling to his boss over his shoulder, "He eats rats and small tarantulas."

"No, he doesn't," Blake called after him. "Iguanas are herbivores."

Great. Chase took one last glance back at them before pushing through the door into the main office area. Blake was currently scratching the lizard under the chin, just how he liked, and Henry leaned into the touch like a reptile in love. Of course Blake would know all the right things to do for Henry. They were perfect for each other.

He shook his head and walked into the office, his lips quirking up in a smile.

Who's the matchmaker now?

11

Promptly at ten that night, Shelby stood outside the employee entrance near the back lot of the Lucky Ace Casino. From where she rested against the cool brick wall she could see the bus stop at the corner. She'd guessed from Chase's arrival that morning at Rockford Security that he didn't have a car of his own yet and that made sense, given his recent parole. There was something about his determined use of public transportation that increased her respect for him, something about him living his life and pushing ahead against all odds that showed his integrity and made her trust him a tad more. After all, he had as much, if not more, on the line here than she did. If things went south again, he would lose everything and end up right back in prison where he'd started. And prison, she imagined, was a hellish place to be.

Minutes later, a bus belched to a stop at the corner and the doors squeaked open. Chase jogged down the steps and caught sight of her immediately, raising his hand in greeting. Her heart raced despite her vow to remain unaffected. Never mind that she thought he might kiss her in the elevator earlier today or that maybe she was disappointed that he didn't. This was business and nothing but business.

He strode up to her and grinned as she took in his appearance. He looked like something out of a bad seventies cop drama. Black shirt, black pants, black knit skull cap which she suspected had a ski mask attached. "What in the world are you wearing?"

"What?" He gave her an affronted look. "I didn't want to be seen."

"Good luck with that now, Starsky." She rolled her eyes at his confused look. "You know, Starsky and Hutch? Seventies cop show?"

When he still seemed perplexed, she snatched the hat off his head and stuffed it into the pocket of his black jacket. "There. At least you don't stand out quite as much. C'mon, let's go."

"Like you're one to talk, Ms. Gloved Hands."

"I've got my reasons, all right?" She used her security badge to buzz them in the back door, then led him through the service halls toward the casino floor. She knew this maze like the back of her hand. Hell, this used to be her playpen when she was a kid. They ducked out into the casino proper, into the same hall where her dad's office was located. She pulled out her security badge again and opened the door.

"Hey, wait a minute." Chase grabbed her arm, his voice low and gruff and sexy as hell. "I thought we were going to Katherine's condo."

"I need to stop here first." She wrenched her arm from his grip and carefully maneuvered through the yellow police tape to get inside. Thankfully, everything looked the same as the last time she'd been in here. Chase entered behind her and moved to turn on the lights, but she stopped him. "No. We don't want anyone to see a light on under the door."

"How are we supposed to move around, huh? Spontaneous Night Vision?"

"I know where I'm going, okay? Just stay here."

Drawing on years of memories, Shelby hurried across the room to the desk and the safe hidden beneath it. She dialed in the code and tried the door. Nothing. Took a deep breath and tried again. Still nada. *Shit.*

Shit, shit, shit. "Someone must've changed the

combination."

"What?" Chase headed toward her, mumbling curses as he bumped into the desk on his way to her side. He knelt close behind her and whispered, "What's going on?"

"Nothing. Just give me a minute." Scowling, she tried to determine what the combination might've been changed to. Katherine had to have been the one who'd done it. What would she choose? Birthday? She dialed in the numbers, but no luck. Their wedding anniversary? Nope. What else? What day could possibly hold that much meaning for her step-monster?

Black certainty settled over her. Of course. It made perfect sense.

Shelby entered the day of her dad's death and heard the satisfying click as the tumblers fell into place. The thick steel door *cha-chunked* open and Shelby fumbled inside her nylon jacket pocket for the copy of the will that had been delivered to her door the night before then stuffed it into the bottom of the safe before closing the thing up once more.

Let the bitch discover I'm on to her.

She smiled in the darkness and scooted back, only to collide with Chase who hovered behind her like a nervous old lady.

"Seriously?" he growled. "What in the hell are you doing?"

"I left the fake will in there for Katherine to find, that's all. She's already been in here and changed the combination but if she leads the cops in here, she'll be in for a real surprise. Might make her do something stupid." She crawled away from him, away from temptation, and stood. "Let's go."

"Huh, good idea."

She took his hand and led him toward the door.

"Hold on," Chase said.

"What?"

"It's weird she'd change the combination on the safe, but not the code to access the office, right? I mean why do one without the other?"

"I don't know. Probably because she'd have to go through casino security to have the main access code changed. Maybe she didn't want to go through the trouble. Or maybe she thought they'd say no, or ask too many questions. Who knows why she does any of the things she does?" She pulled on his hand and this time he followed. "C'mon. We need to get up to the condo before she gets back."

They slipped through the police tape once more and Shelby closed the door behind them then pulled off her gloves. "Okay. Let's do it."

"Wait." Chase took her arm once more. "We need to make sure those video cameras are off. I think Owen Rockford can help us with that. Where's his office?"

"At the end of the hall. But he's probably in the main control room at this time of night. That's on the other side of the casino. I'll show you." She laced her fingers with his, partly to make sure they didn't get separated and partly because it just felt good, and led him through a maze of slot machines and gaming tables. From the special performance area near the main bar, the sounds of her favorite country song drifted through the air. "Oh! I forgot Jan Winters is playing here tonight. The shortcut goes right behind the stage, maybe we can catch a glimpse."

Chase pulled back. "Wait a minute ... I don't know if—"

"Come on, it'll be fine. It's just a shortcut, I do it all the time."

She dragged him through the heavy black curtains covering the entrance to the bar then up a side aisle toward the backstage area. She'd used this shortcut hundreds of times, rubbing elbows with the various stars that played at the casino. She never stopped to talk to them though, never used her 'status' of the casino owner's daughter to get a private audience. She wasn't like that.

Still, she had to admit, she did get a little thrill running around backstage. But tonight that thrill was overshadowed by the serious job they had in front of them.

She snuck them behind several burly-looking bodyguards and up a narrow wooden set of stairs to the wings of the stage. In the shadows of the curtains, she spotted Jan Winters—resplendent in a white sequined gown and diamonds, standing close to a dark-haired, handsome man.

"Uh-oh," Chase hesitated.

Shelby frowned at him. "What?"

"Chase? Chase Evans!" The man hurried over and pulled an embarrassed Chase into a bro hug. "Blake told me you finally rejoined the world. Welcome back, man!"

"Thanks, Dino" Chase said to the man, then hugged Jan who had come to join them.

"It's good to see you, man," Dino said. "You look really good."

"Good to see you too," Chase said. Before she knew it, he'd tugged Shelby forward to his side right in front of Jan Winters. She was momentarily starstruck, her face hot and her cheeks aching from the goofy, nervous smile she now had plastered to her face. "And this is Shelby Bryant. My...uh... friend."

"Nice to meet you, Shelby." Jan shook her hand warmly. "I'm so sorry about your dad."

"Thank you." She surprised herself by getting any words out past her tight vocal cords. "I love your work. You're my favorite singer."

"Aw, thank you." Jan put her arm around Shelby and squeezed. "Listen, I lost my dad too, when I was little. If you need someone to talk to, please feel free to call me. Chase knows how to get ahold of me."

She couldn't imagine ever being un-starstruck enough to girl-talk with Jan Winters, but she appreciated the offer anyway. "I'll keep that in mind. Thanks for the offer."

"I mean it. Any friend of Chase's is a friend of mine."

Dino shook her hand next, his grip as tough as his persona, but his grin friendly. "So, I hear Blake is responsible for you two getting together, huh?"

"What?" Chase said. His body tensed beside her. "No. There is no *us two*." He gestured quickly between himself and Shelby before dropping his arm from around her waist. "And don't believe everything you hear around the office either."

"Right." Dino kissed Jan's hand and pulled her close to him again, obviously head-over-heels in love with her. "Well, it wouldn't be the first time old Blake played matchmaker."

"Yeah, I heard." Chase took Shelby's hand and started to pull her away. "Well, we best get going."

"It was so great to see you again, Chase. Really. And so great meeting you, Shelby," Jan said. "Hey, are you guys coming to the family dinner on Sunday?"

"I'll be there," Chase said. "Seeing as how I'm staying with Blake right now and all."

"What about you, Shelby?" Dino asked, his smile turning devious as he glanced back at Chase. "You should bring her along, man. It'll be fun."

"We'll see. Later, guys." Chase hightailed it out of there, with Shelby in tow, before she could say a word.

Once they were back out on the casino floor again, she pulled free, glancing back over her shoulder. "What was *that* about? What family dinner?"

"It's this thing the Rockfords do. The whole clan descends on Blake's house on a Sunday and shake the rafters with all their collective chaos."

"Oh." She frowned. "You live with Blake?"

"Right now, yeah. It was either that or a halfway house while I finished my parole. This is way better, believe me. Blake helped negotiate it with my parole officer."

"Wow. That's nice of him."

"Yeah, he's really got my back." He rubbed a hand across the nape of his neck. "Too much, sometimes, in fact."

A thought occurred to Shelby, one that made her heart sink. "Crap. I forgot about your parole. You won't get in trouble for being out so late, will you?"

"Nah. Not if I'm careful, and if I don't make a habit of it. But let's hurry just in case and get to that control room. We need to find something on Katherine so this whole night isn't a complete bust."

"ARE you sure he's here tonight?" Chase asked as they arrived in a small, empty office. *Damn.* He was counting on getting help with those cameras and Blake had assured him his cousin Owen would be sympathetic to their cause.

"Yeah, it's Friday. He's scheduled to work every weekend night. It's our busiest time." Shelby pulled him inside then let go of his hand. He felt chilled without the contact. "Maybe he's in the camera room."

Chase followed her across the short space to another door near the corner. Inside sat a guy with dark hair and broad shoulders, scowling at a wall full of monitors and looking completely bored by them all.

Shelby knocked on the door then flashed her most endearing smile. "Hi, Owen. Got a minute?"

The dude swiveled in his chair then stood, showing off the impressive height and good-looks all the Rockfords seemed blessed with. "For you Shelby? Always." His warm brown gaze shifted to Chase and lit with surprise. "Chase Evans? How you doing, my man? So great to see you!"

They shared a brief bro hug before stepping away again. "I'm really good. Thanks for asking. And thanks for giving me the job here at the casino, even if it didn't work out."

Shelby gave Chase an irritated look and whispered under her breath, "Do you know everyone who works for Rockford Security?"

Chase laughed. "Only the ones who are related."

"Which means, yeah," Owen chimed in, helpful as always. "He does."

Shelby's cheeks flushed a delightful shade of rose, and Chase couldn't help pulling her close once more as Owen continued. "So Chase. Seems you got yourself in quite a pickle right out of the gate. What's up with that, huh?" He turned to Shelby, his handsome face growing somber. "I'm truly sorry for what happened to your father. He was a good man."

"Thanks." She tucked her hair behind her ear and looked away.

She trembled beneath Chase's arm and seeing her so vulnerable tore him up inside. He gave her a tight squeeze for strength. "Um, you know the police seem to consider me a suspect, right?"

"Yeah, Blake mentioned it. Saw something on the news too. But who believes anything they've got to say." Owen chuckled.

"Don't let Laura hear you say that," Chase warned. "She'll kick your ass."

"I know, right?" Owen grinned. "So, why am I getting this visit?"

"Well." Chase tightened his grip on Shelby, more for his own moral support than hers. "I don't trust the police to do their job, so I'm looking for something to clear my name."

"What can I do to help?"

Shelby looked up then, her expression determined, all traces of sorrow gone. "We need to search Katherine's condo, without being taped. Can you help us with that?"

Chase smiled, pride welling within him. There was that backbone he admired so much.

Owen took a step back, hands raised. "I did not hear

you just ask me that, Shelby." He inched closer to the camera control panel on the wall. "In fact, I didn't see you two here at all tonight." His shoulder bumped against one set of buttons, shutting them off. A label above them read Bryant Condo. "I'm, uh, going to take my usual fifteen-minute walk around the casino floor now and make sure Jan and Dino have everything they need. By the way, those cameras are *not* off now." He nodded and winked. "They will *not* be back online in twenty minutes."

"Uh, thanks, man," Chase said as Owen walked toward the exit. "I owe you one."

"You owe me dozens." He grinned and waved to Shelby then disappeared out a nearby service entrance.

"C'mon. Let's go." Shelby pulled him back to the elevators, and they rode up to the condo in record time. "Twenty minutes isn't as long as it sounds."

Once inside, she headed straight for the table and drawer they'd seen that morning in the tapes. Shelby pulled her gloves back on and opened it. "Damn, nothing."

"Shit." Chase reached into his pocket and pulled out another pair of latex gloves he'd stashed there earlier. "What about the phone? Maybe we can find the one she was using. Those SIM cards keep track of all kinds of data."

He riffled through drawer after drawer, but only found several iPhone cases. One of the other phones he'd seen her with on the tapes looked like a cheap Nokia with a flashy case, but he didn't find anything like that.

"Do you think Katherine has an accomplice?" Shelby straightened from her spot on the floor before a large mahogany credenza. "Bank statements might show something, if she made payments to them or suspicious withdrawals of cash."

"Maybe. I don't know." Chase sighed. "She's smart. If she *is* paying somebody, she'd most likely do it in small, untraceable amounts, over weeks or months, not days."

Shelby walked over and slumped onto the sofa. She scowled, then dug beneath the cushions. "Something's poking me. What the..." She pulled out the burner Nokia phone he'd seen in the footage that morning. "Oh. Is this the device you were looking for?"

He frowned recognizing the fake bling glued all over its hideous pink cover. "That's it ... seems odd she would have it stuffed in the cushions."

"She's a ditz, it probably fell out of one of her Gucci bags and she couldn't find it." Shelby clicked it on and scrolled through the screens while Chase took a seat beside her. "Now where is the call history?"

"I'll find it." He snatched the phone from her hands before she could protest. "With those big old things covering your hands you couldn't find anything."

"Hey, Mr. I'm-Going-To-Dress-Like-A-Bad-Guy-Stereotype. You've got no room to talk."

"Here it is." He grinned as she flipped him off, then quickly frowned. "Crap."

"What's wrong?"

"The whole history's been wiped. No calls, no texts. The only number in here is named 'My Boo <3'".

"Well," Shelby reached for the phone again. "Let's call it and find out who it is."

"Forget it." His stomach swooped as he stared at the phone. "It's my number."

How the hell had Katherine managed to get his new cell number? He'd barely had time to memorize the damned thing himself since he'd just gotten it at the store the day after his release.

"Wait, so there really is something going on between you?" The sad betrayed look in Shelby's eyes pierced his heart.

"No. I have no idea how she got my number." Chase grabbed her hand. "You believe me don't you?"

Her eyes softened and he felt like he'd won the lottery. She *did* believe him. But then the gravity of the situation hit him. "Shit. No wonder this was so easy to find. She wanted someone to find it. She's—"

The sound of the elevator gears grinding interrupted him. They both turned in unison.

"Crap. Someone's coming," Chase said.

"Follow me." Shelby grabbed his hand and pulled him over to a small coat closet near the front entrance, then tugged him in beside her. With the door closed, it was a tight squeeze at best. They were pressed against each other like sardines and his pulse pounded loud in his ears, obliterating everything except the dark and the warmth of Shelby's body and his untimely overwhelming urge to kiss her.

Bad idea. The adrenaline coursing through his veins drowned out the sound of whoever had entered the condo. He had to remain silent, lest he was caught violating curfew. He couldn't see Shelby, only feel her. And if he was destined to find himself mired up Shit's Creek anyway... He leaned down, finding Shelby's mouth and swallowing her gasp.

The door flew open and blinding light flashed into their small, private heaven. Chase squinted into the glare and did his best to hide Shelby.

"Well, hello there," Katherine said, her smile as smug as her tone.

Chase shifted position to ease the pressure off his aching butt. Once more, there he was, stuck in an uncomfortable metal chair in a dingy interrogation room at the Las Vegas PD. *Dammit it all to hell and back.* He should've known Katherine had set up that whole scene—taped herself putting the money in the drawer, stuffing that ugly ass burner phone between the couch cushions—knowing he and Shelby would come investigating when they saw the footage.

He'd been so stupid.

He scrubbed a hand over his face. Apparently five years in the slammer had done nothing to improve his sleuthing skills whatsoever.

The door behind him creaked open then closed with a resounding *thwack*. Detective Moore once more took a seat across from him. Her suit was different today—black, with a white shirt beneath—but her no-nonsense expression remained the same as always. She folded her hands atop the same manila file with his name and mug shot across the front and stared at him without blinking, her smile not reaching her ebony eyes.

Well, this should be fun. Not.

"Mr. Evans, we have Shelby in the other room. She'll turn on you, sooner rather than later. Don't kid yourself."

Chase crossed his arms and did his best to hide the tension knotted in his gut. "I doubt it. Why would she? We didn't kill her father."

Besides, sweet little Shelby wouldn't turn on me. Would she?

"Murder or not, I have you both on trespassing charges and you, specifically, Mr. Evans for breaking curfew. That's enough to send you back to jail." Her smile increased, showing even white teeth bright against her dark skin. "Now, something tells me prison isn't someplace you'd like to revisit."

He played along, flashing his own small grin. "You're right, Detective. But tell the truth. You want me for the murder charge, not this crap. You want the big kahuna, the career-making, national-news-worthy indictment. Truth is, putting me away for those little things steals your thunder. Sorry, but I'm not biting." He sat forward and mimicked her body language, a trick he learned in law school to gain another's trust and support. "I didn't do it."

Moore, apparently not buying into his psychological cues, sat back and reached into her pocket. "Explain this then, Mr. Evans."

She slid the burner phone across the table to him.

He didn't touch the hideous thing, just sat back himself, once more mirroring his interrogator. "Looks like a cheap, tacky piece of shit to me."

"It's registered to Shelby Bryant."

"Huh." *Well, shit.* Didn't expect that tidbit of new information. He scrambled to come up with a credible lie. "It's not hers. It's mine."

"Yours, huh? Interesting." Moore reached over and grabbed the sparkly fuchsia nightmare and clicked it on, then thumbed through several screens. "You always list your own cell number as 'My Boo'?"

"Sure." He narrowed his gaze and gave a half smile. "As Whitney has always said, learning to love yourself is the greatest love of all, right?"

"I see." Moore's tone suggested that she saw straight through his horseshit.

Chase pushed to his feet and slid his chair back

under the table. "Well, if there's nothing else you need from me, Detective, I should really get home before my boss worries."

"Sit down, Mr. Evans." The steel in her voice brooked no argument. "Leave now and I'll book you on the trespassing charge so fast your damn fool head will spin right off."

He sat.

"Let's see." Moore flipped open the file and pulled out several sheets of paper which she passed to him. "Have a look at those. Care to explain?"

Sharp pain pounded against his temples as he stared at the papers. "I've never seen these before."

"Really? Seems to me a guy like you would remember a pretty girl like Shelby sending you e-mails in prison."

"What? No." He scrunched his nose and thrust the sheets back at her. "Believe me, I would've known if someone like Shelby Bryant tried to contact me."

"Yeah, that's what I think too." She gathered the e-mails and placed them back in the file. "So, tell me, Mr. Evans. Is this when you guys hatched your plan to murder Warren Bryant?"

"Shit." Chase pressed the heels of his hands hard against his eyes. "I told you I had nothing to do with that. I didn't kill Warren Bryant, nor did I make any plans with anyone to do him harm."

"Hmm." Moore steepled her fingers and tapped them against her full lips. "These correspondences suggest otherwise. Perhaps your girlfriend Shelby was frustrated over her money troubles and her daddy refused to help."

Damn. He'd never gotten any emails in prison and he was positive Shelby never sent him any. She didn't even know him then and she wouldn't send shit like this—she couldn't care less about money. But who then? Katherine? Maybe. She'd set them up in the condo, the emails were probably just one more layer of her evil plan.

One thing was certain. Moore wouldn't buy into his theory without proof, which she didn't have. Not yet anyway. And continuing on this path would only dig his hole deeper, so he switched tactics. Always keep the opposition on their toes. Something else he learned in law school. He sat forward and clasped his hands atop the table. "Tell me, Detective. Did I ever answer any of these e-mails?"

Moore didn't answer, but her red-painted lips thinned slightly.

Bingo.

Chase resisted the urge to gloat over his small

victory and instead charged forward while his momentum was good. "That's what I thought. So, if Shelby sent them, then I guess I must've missed them. All what?" He squinted at the folder. "Twenty of them?"

Seemingly undeterred, Moore pushed on. "I'm supposed to believe it's a coincidence you two are friends now?"

"Not a coincidence at all. In fact, you can thank my boss Blake Rockford for introducing us. He's the one who gave me the Lucky Ace assignment, though I never got a chance to meet Warren Bryant, much less kill him."

Moore took a deep breath, a hard glint in her midnight dark eyes. "Wow. Interesting you'd start a new job, but never meet with your client?"

"Nope. Never got the chance. He was Blakes's client, I was just the hired help."

"Listen, I appreciate your inventiveness, Mr. Evans, but let's cut through the bullshit, okay? We have proof you were in there, in Bryant's office. If you confess now and tell us all about what happened, we'll go easy. Promise."

Proof I was in Bryant's office? No way. She had to be bluffing. Fishing just like she had been with those emails. He'd been careful. Both times. Still, he needed to find out what they did have if he had any hopes of figuring a way out of this mess. "Did Katherine take something else of mine while she was trying to seduce me?"

Moore smiled, all cool confidence and pure menace. "I don't think so. Not this, anyway."

"What?"

"I can't reveal that, Mr. Evans."

She wanted to play things that way, huh? Fine. He could play hardball too, when necessary. "It doesn't matter, Detective. Everything you've got right now is purely circumstantial. It'll take more than that for a conviction, especially murder. And whatever it is you think you found most likely could've been put there by anyone. I was never in Warren Bryant's office on the day of the murder. Check your video surveillance feeds. I'm sure you'll see I left the hotel before he was killed and didn't return."

Moore stared him down across the expanse of the table. Her once stoic expression now looked decidedly annoyed, but Chase refused to say another word. If they brought him in again, he'd get an attorney and really screw up their plans.

After several tense seconds, Detective Moore grabbed the file and left as abruptly as she'd come.

Alone, finally, Chase exhaled and slumped into his

seat. *Goddamn.* He'd been through this shit before but even so, this had been a tough session. He couldn't imagine how poor Shelby was faring down the hall. The bastards probably had her in hysterics by now. And he didn't believe the detective's story for one second. Shelby wouldn't turn on him, no matter what Moore insinuated. Then again, maybe he wasn't such a great judge of character, he'd thought Shane wouldn't turn on him either.

The door behind him opened once more and Chase's whole body went whipcord tight. For Christ's sake, he couldn't seem to catch a break today. Round One with Moore had been bad enough. Round Two without some time to recover might damn near make his head explode.

Except when he looked up, it wasn't the detective's face he saw.

"Get up," Blake said, looking every inch the ex-cop he was. "We're going home."

"Uh, okay." He stood. "They're not arresting me for trespassing or violating parole?"

Didn't think he'd beat those charges, no matter what he'd told Moore. Still, he wasn't about to question his freedom at this point.

"No, they're not." Blake shoved him toward the door and out into the bustling hall beyond. "Because you weren't violating parole. Or trespassing. You were on assignment for Rockford Securities at the Lucky Ace, understand? We had to call in additional people to cover the Jan Winters event. Part of that assignment is making sure the whole building is secure, including the condo." Blake took Chase's arm and dragged him through the station, his icy gaze locked on the entrance ahead and his expression granite tough. "Now get your ass moving. I had to call in a lot of favors to make this work."

They reached the exit in record time and walked out into the brisk night air. Chase took a deep breath and rubbed his sore bicep once Blake let him go. "Thanks, man."

"Thank me at home." He continued on to his car, but Chase didn't move.

"Wait. What about Shelby? She's still in there and—"

"And nothing." Blake punched the button on his key fob and the car's lights blinked on and off as the doors clicked open. "There's nothing we can do for her tonight. She's still in an interrogation room."

"But I—"

"But nothing." Blake opened the driver's side door then leaned his forearms atop the roof of the navy sedan, watching Chase with his lethal blue stare. "I think the two of you have gotten into enough trouble together this evening, don't you? Now please stop being a pain in my ass and get in the car. Shelby will be fine. The detective questioning her is a friend and he'll go easy on her. Besides, she's tougher than she looks."

Resigned, Chase climbed into the passenger seat and secured his seat belt. Blake was right, about Shelby and about all the trouble they'd caused. Still, as they pulled out of the parking lot and headed home to Summerlin, Chase couldn't help running through his conversation with Moore. Clearly those e-mails were fake, but it didn't fit. Why would Katherine imply a prior relationship between him and Shelby? There's no way she could've known Blake planned to offer him that job once he got out. Hell, he hadn't even known. And why would the police believe Shelby would randomly e-mail him in jail then be stupid enough to talk openly about killing her father?

Cursing, he rested his head back against the seat and closed his eyes. Man, he was so damned tired of fighting every single day to prove his innocence, to prove he deserved a second chance, to prove worthy of his freedom. He couldn't do this anymore tonight.

Tomorrow. He'd pick up his weapons and shield and charge into that battle again tomorrow.

For now, though, all he wanted to do was forget and sleep.

* * *

SHELBY FIDDLED with the hem of her sweater for the umpteenth time and glanced at the two people sitting across the square conference table. The man, Detective Troy Atkins, she remembered from that day with Katherine in the condo. He still seemed nice enough—offering her coffee, allowing her time to collect her thoughts, asking her if she was all right. The woman though, Moore—a pretty African American woman with attitude to spare—looked like she'd just as soon lock Shelby up and throw away the key as talk to her. She'd been there that day at the condo too.

Of course, the dark shadows lurking in the corners of the room and stale air that smelled of floor wax and bad decisions didn't help either. Ever since she'd discovered her dad's *extracurricular* activities at the Lucky Ace as a teenager, Shelby had nightmares about just this kind of scenario. Being dragged into an interrogation room and questioned with no hope of escape, even though she was innocent.

Guilt by association.

Her chest constricted and her stomach churned and she took a deep breath to keep calm.

"Tell me about these." Detective Moore slid a manila folder across the table to her.

Shelby frowned and opened the file, staring down at the printed e-mails stuffed inside. "Um, I didn't write these, if that's what you're asking."

Moore sat forward while Detective Atkins remained motionless, silent. "They were sent to Chase Evans in prison. Each one is time and date stamped."

"Y-yes." Shelby blinked down at the papers in front of her, her legs trembling. "I see that."

"And they're from your e-mail address."

"I didn't send these. I swear." She met Detective Moore's gaze. "I never even met Chase Evans until after my dad died."

"Right." Moore nodded. "And where did you say you met him again?"

"At my dad's casino, the Lucky Ace."

"So you just met him, and you decided it was a good idea to become romantically involved with the man who may have killed your father?"

"What? No!" She raised a trembling hand and pushed her long blond curls behind her ear. "It isn't like that."

"What is it like then, Miss Bryant?" Moore sat back and crossed her arms. "Please, enlighten me."

Shelby glanced at Atkins, but his gaze remained steadfast on his coffee cup, frowning. She desperately wanted to bite her fingernails, a habit she'd broken way back in tenth grade, but she also didn't want this Detective Moore to know how upset she was. Showing her emotions wouldn't do her any favors in this situation. She cleared her throat. "First off, I don't believe that Chase Evans killed my dad."

"Really? And how do you know that?"

"I just know. I think he's being set up."

"Set up?" Atkins sat up a little straighter. "By who?"

"I'm not sure yet."

"I see." Moore snorted. "This is a gut feeling of yours then, huh? What about the sex between him and your stepmother? That's a set up too?"

Shelby didn't answer. Did the cops really think Chase and Katherine had had sex? They had seen the same video Shelby had and it was pretty clear by the timestamps that nothing happened. Were they just trying to get her upset? Probably. She wasn't going to bite, though. She was afraid that no matter what she said they'd twist it and use it against her ... or Chase. Not to mention that she didn't want to admit—especially to herself— how much she was really starting to like Chase.

Moore toyed with the folder and smiled. "It was smart of you, you know. Brilliant, really. To use his urge for revenge to get what you want."

Exhausted, Shelby did her best to follow the detective's line of thought and failed. "I'm sorry?"

"Then you didn't tell Chase that it was your dad who tipped off the police about the drugs stashed in his apartment? Interesting. I mean the force always suspected someone operated a trafficking ring out of the casino, then your father was helpful enough to hand us the right address on a silver platter. Vegas has him to thank for one of the biggest drug busts in Nevada history. Nice work."

Bile stung Shelby's throat and she swallowed hard. She'd known Chase's conviction was drug related, but not that her dad had been involved. Chase must've known though, wouldn't he? Wouldn't it have come out as part of his trial? Yet he'd never said a word. She took a deep breath and squeezed her eyes shut. Okay, so maybe he did have additional motive to kill her dad.

And maybe she didn't know him at all. Not really.

"Hey." Moore looked at Atkins then back at Shelby. "I think we'll just give you some time to consider all this." She stood and walked to the door, the heels of her black pumps clacking loud against the linoleum floor. "I'll be back soon."

Shelby held it together until the door slammed behind Detective Moore, then tears formed against her will. Atkins reached across the table and patted her hand. "You want some more coffee?"

She stared at the untouched, now cold, cup in front of her. Throat clogged, she shrugged in response.

"Okay, great. I'll be right back with fresh brew." He picked up her cup and left the room.

Alone with her thoughts, Shelby swiped the back of her hand under her eyes. She wanted to find Chase and demand he tell her the truth, the whole truth, and nothing but the truth. Then again, how could she possibly believe him now when he'd apparently been dishonest with her from the start. She sat forward and rested her forearms on the table, dropping her head down on top of them. God things were such a mess.

Detective Atkins returned a few moments later. "Sorry that took so long. Had to wait on a fresh pot." She raised her head and looked at the cup of steaming liquid he set in front of her. He smiled at her, not the icy affair Moore flashed, but one that seemed genuine and kind. "I put cream and sugar in it too, like you requested before. Not that it makes it great or anything, but the caffeine will help you stay awake."

She wrapped her cold fingers around the warm cup and sighed. "Thanks, Detective Atkins."

"You're welcome. And please, call me Troy." He sat across from her again and took a long swig of coffee. "So, I'm puzzled. What does a pretty, smart, sweet girl like you see in a guy like Evans?"

Heat prickled her cheeks and she looked away. Detective Troy Atkins was quite a catch—handsome, great job, funny, nice. All awesome things in her book. Except for one problem. She'd met Chase Evans first and now the guy seemed to consume her every waking thought, especially since they'd teamed up to find her dad's real murderer. Besides, it was getting involved with good looking men who were nice to her that got her into this interrogation room in the first place.

When she remained silent, Troy continued. "Hey, I understand if you made a mistake. We all do sometimes when it comes to love."

Yep. A mistake. That was a perfect description of her choice to make out with Chase in her stepmonster's closet. Biggest, dumbest mistake ever.

"You let your emotions carry you away," he said. "You don't mean for it to happen."

Got that right, buddy.

"Listen, Shelby. All we're trying to do here is catch the bad guy, whoever that may be. Honestly, I don't think that's you. But if you do know who it is, then you have to tell us, even if Chase Evans is your partner in crime."

"Like I said, Chase and I aren't working together."

Disappointment crossed Troy's face before he hid it. "You were mad at your dad, Shelby. It happens. And we all do stupid things when we're mad. Don't let one stupid mistake ruin the rest of your life. Please. We can cut you a deal."

"I wasn't mad at my dad. I loved him. And even if I was mad, I wouldn't kill him." The mention of her father had her vision blurring with tears again.

"Then why did you send him these, Shelby?"

He pulled some new papers out of the folder and passed them to her. She sniffled and squinted at the handwritten notes, petty things threatening her dad if he didn't buy her what she wanted or pay more attention to her. She shook her head. She would never, ever say things like that to her dad. Ever. But damn if the handwriting didn't look eerily similar to hers.

Icy dread trickled down her spine. Whoever was doing this was good. Too good.

She pushed the paper back to Troy with a shaky hand. "I didn't write those either."

"Shelby," he said, his tone infinitely patient. "We

compared these to a sample of your handwriting. Statistically they are a good match."

Righteous anger flared alongside her despair. "Dammit, I'm telling you these aren't from me. I don't know where you got them, but I didn't write them, okay?"

Tiredness, combined with overwhelming stress, finally crumbled her last defenses and she broke down in sobs. "T-those st-tupid n-notes don't even make sense. Why would I kill my dad if I wanted more time with him, huh?" Nose running and eyes streaming, she looked across at Troy. "Now I'll never get to spend time with him again. Never." She hiccupped and took the tissue Troy handed her. "Can't you people understand? I loved Dad. I'd do anything to spend just one more day with him. Anything."

13

———

From the guest room on the second floor, Chase heard the ruckus downstairs and his anxiety ratcheted higher. Sure, he hung out with some of the Rockfords at work, but this was different. This was a family get-together and the last thing he wanted to be on that dreary, late-autumn Sunday was an interloper.

The smell of meat roasting and veggies baking made his stomach rumble and he inched closer to the top of the stairs. Blake had insisted he come down, partake of the food and the camaraderie, but Chase wasn't so sure. It was one thing to be nice to him because he was an employee. It was another to hang out with an ex-con on the weekends for shits and giggles.

Henry snuggled in closer to the side of his neck, as

if for encouragement, and Chase glanced sideways at the green guy. Blake had taken a real shine to him, but insisted Chase spend as much time with the iguana as he did, saying they'd bonded already or some nonsense. While Chase would deny it until he was blue in the face, he'd missed Henry. "Hey, buddy. What do you think? Should we go get some grub?"

Henry flicked his tongue out against Chase's cheek.

"Okay, then. Let's do this." He took a deep breath for courage and descended the steps. Blake saw him before he reached the bottom floor. He raised a hand and waved Chase over to the busy living room.

Chase waved back and weaved through the crowd of Rockford siblings and cousins and God knew who else. He nodded to people he recognized and kept his head down with those he didn't.

Logan Rockford toasted Chase with his beer as he stopped beside Blake, then recoiled once he spotted Henry. "Hey, keep that beast away from me, man."

"Seriously, Logan?" Blake said. "After some of the women you've dated, Henry's a vast improvement."

"Whatever, man." He took a long swig of beer and a step back, eyeing the iguana suspiciously. "He's got that look, like he wants to gnaw my face off."

Blake snorted then leaned over and tickled Henry

under the chin. "Are you having fun with your Uncle Chase, huh? Who's Daddy's good boy, huh? Who? That's right, Henry. Henry's Blake's good boy, aren't you?"

Logan gave a disgusted groan. "Ew. You treat that thing like it's your kid or something, bro. Seriously, ew."

"Henry's a sentient being, just like you." Blake turned and glared at his younger brother, The Hurt in full force. "Besides, you're going to hurt his feelings."

"Right." Logan shook his head and backed away, his expression dripping with wary disgust. "I'll just call and book you a room at the loony bin, bro. Arriving tomorrow okay?"

"Hey, Chase!" Laura Rockford came up beside him. She had her arm around her new boyfriend—Mike McQuade, maybe—if Chase remembered correctly. Some computer geek turned billionaire. Not exactly his thing, but to each his own. Laura leaned in and smiled at Henry. "So this is the new pet you got for my brother, huh?"

"Yep. This is Henry." Chase glanced at Blake and smiled. "More payback than pet."

"He seems to be enjoying himself," Mike said.

"Yeah, he's a good boy, aren't you, my man?" Chase turned and made kissy noises at Henry.

Logan sighed loud. "That's it. I'm outta here. Gotta find me some sane folks to hang with."

"Good luck with that around here," Laura called to Logan's retreating back, then turned to run a finger over Henry's head. "You know Logan's the one who's terrified of lizards, not Blake, right?"

"Yeah, figured that one out a bit too late. Bad planning on my part." He leaned in a bit closer to Laura, taking advantage of the fact Blake and Mike had gotten into a deep discussion about new emerging technology in the security field, and whispered, "What should I have gotten to scare Blake?"

Laura glanced up at him and winked. "A committed relationship."

"Oh." *Well, damn.* He couldn't handle one of those himself, let alone for someone else. Not for the first time that day, Chase's thoughts drifted to Shelby. It had been three days since their awful night in the LVPD interrogation room and he hoped she was okay. Leaving her there might've been the only option, but it still felt like a shitty thing to do. He'd texted her several times to apologize and see if she was okay, but had received no answer. He couldn't blame her, but he felt sad that their short partnership was over now. He'd have to figure out how to clear himself all alone.

Uncomfortable, he shuffled his feet and focused

on his conversation with Laura. "Wasn't Blake married before?"

"Yeah, but she died in the line of duty. He's never gotten over it."

Laura squeezed Mike tight around the waist and cuddled into his side while Chase clutched Henry's leash tighter. He couldn't imagine how that must have felt. Another reason to avoid relationships even if his thoughts did keep returning to Shelby.

A commotion sounded behind him and he turned with the rest of the crowd to see Blake's mother, Pearl Rockford enter the room from the direction of the kitchen. He'd never actually met either of Blake's parents, but Blake always talked about them like they were royalty or something. He inched back farther toward the wall behind him, not wanting to interrupt their family reunion, as Pearl made her way around the room, greeting and embracing everyone.

She stopped in front of Chase—all bright smile and sleek silver hair, still vibrant and attractive despite her age—and smiled broadly. "Finally, I get to meet the illustrious Chase Evans. Blake's told me so many wonderful things about you over the years. And I see you brought a friend too."

Henry jumped from Chase's shoulder up onto the

fireplace mantel beside him as Pearl leaned in and kissed Chase on both cheeks then hugged him tight.

Stunned, Chase patted her on the back, staring after the woman as she moved on down the line of guests. He'd expected the other Rockfords to be polite, but that was about it. So far, they'd welcomed him with open arms. He couldn't remember the last time he'd felt so accepted. It felt good. Better than he wanted to admit.

The doorbell rang and Chase took ahold of Henry's leash again, not wanting him to run out the door. Logan answered it then stepped back and scanned the crowd before pointing back in Chase's general direction.

"Hey, man. There's someone here to see you," Logan called above the din.

People parted and Chase froze in place as Shelby came into view.

***

SHELBY HELD her breath while all eyes seemed to turn in her direction.

Crap. She should've remembered what Dino Machiavelli had said the other night at the casino. Today was Blake Rockford's family dinner. She hadn't meant to interrupt, but it was too late now. Besides, this was the only day when she had a few hours free from the shelter.

They had unfinished business to discuss.

She followed Logan Rockford across the packed living room to where Chase stood near the fireplace, looking both adorable and guilty as hell. And considering the last time they'd seen each other, he should feel guilty. Especially after the way he'd bailed on her at the police station. She'd looked for him once they'd finally released her shortly after midnight, but was told he'd taken off a few hours earlier with Blake.

As she got closer to Chase, she noticed Henry perched on the fireplace mantel, basking in a ray of sunlight streaming through the clouds outside. At least one of them felt at ease at the moment.

"Hey," she said once Logan left them alone again. Well, if you considered standing in the middle of at least thirty people "alone". "Uh, I wondered if we could talk."

"Sure." The word emerged as little more than a gruff grunt. Chase coughed and tried again. "Um, sure."

Someone nearby called out then toasted someone else. The sound of clanking glass and the smell of spilled alcohol filled the air.

"Is there someplace more quiet?" she asked.

"Yeah, of course." He took her arm and lead her toward a doorway near where she'd entered the two-story home. She glanced around as they weaved through the crowd. The place was nice, modern and decorated in a southwestern style she liked. Homey, yet clean and professional, like Blake Rockford himself. It suited him.

Chase led her toward the back of the house and through a pair of sliding glass doors out onto a deserted patio in the back. "This work?"

"This is fine." She hunkered down inside her hoodie, more for security than protection against the elements. Even this late in October and overcast, the temperature during the height of the day was still close to seventy. "So."

"So." He crossed his arms and leaned a shoulder against the stucco wall. "Hey, uh, before we get started, I wanted you to know I'm sorry about leaving the station without you. Blake showed up and whisked me out of there before I even knew what the hell was going on. I tried to text you afterward to make sure you were okay, but I guess they didn't go through. Sorry."

She crossed her arms too, more to keep from reaching out to him and hugging away his forlorn look than anything else. Time for the truth. "They went through. I just needed some time before I was ready to face you again."

"Is this because of what happened in the closet at Katherine's?"

"No." Shelby sighed. Sure, the kiss played a part, but that wasn't why they needed to talk. *Courage, girl. You can do this.* "Why didn't you tell me about what really happened between you and my dad?"

"What do you mean?" Chase frowned, his gray eyes wary. "I never met your father."

Her shoulders slumped. He was still going to deny it, even after what the police had told her. Frustrated, Shelby jabbed a finger into his chest. She wanted him to look at her, wanted him to explain himself, wanted to get some kind of goddamned reaction out of him other than cold indifference. "You might not have met him, but you knew of him. What about all that 'trusting each other' bullshit back at the casino, huh? That we're partners?" She laughed, the sound unpleasant even to her own ears. "Except you forgot to tell me one gigantic thing—that you *did* have real motive to kill my dad. I mean, who wouldn't want revenge on someone for taking away five years of their life, huh?"

"What?" Chase looked genuinely surprised. "What are you talking about?"

Was it possible Chase really didn't know that drug bust had stemmed from her father? Or was he playing her for a fool? She had to find out. "My father tipped off the cops that all those drugs were stashed at your house. Are you trying to tell me you have no idea who blew the whistle on you back then? Seems far-fetched to me."

Crimson dotted his cheeks. "So that's it? You think I'm lying? How the hell would I know who blew the whistle? The police usually don't name their informants or those informants don't live long. In the trial the police just said they got intel from someone high up in the organization. I assumed it was an undercover cop or something. You mean it was your dad?"

Shelby's anger deflated. It made perfect sense, they would have had to keep her Dad's name secret otherwise those drug dealers would have taken revenge. Here she was thinking he had lied and kept things from her. She'd blasted in here so sure he was being an asshole and it turned out that *she* was the asshole for doubting him.

"The cops said you knew. That it gave you motive to take revenge on my dad. That you might have killed him because he was the reason you went to prison," she said weakly jabbing her finger at his chest again to punctuate the word 'you'.

Chase grabbed her hand. His voice softened. "The cops told you that on purpose, to try to get us to turn on each other. But Shelby, whether or not it was your dad who tipped off the cops, it wasn't his fault I went to prison, okay? It was..." He took a deep breath. "It was my brother's, all right?"

"Your brother's?" Stunned, she didn't even try to pull her hand away. "I didn't know you had a brother."

"Yeah, I do." He laced his fingers with hers and led her over to a large rattan chaise lounge set off to the side of the patio, away from the view of the people inside. They took a seat and he kept her hand in his, holding it loosely between his open knees. "I'll tell you the truth, if you want. But you can't tell a soul. Especially not Blake or the police. Understand?"

She nodded, afraid to say anything lest she scare him away.

"Okay." He scowled down at their joined hands, tracing his thumb over her knuckles absently as he spoke. "The heroin at the apartment most likely did come from the Lucky Ace. That's probably how your father knew where to find it. But like I said, it wasn't mine." He scooted closer to her on the seat. "Hell, I've never done drugs in my life, other than a bit of pot back in high school, but who doesn't right?"

Shelby squeezed his hand. "You went to prison and—"

"I don't expect you to understand, Shelby, but my brother, Shane, had a hard life. It's my fault." He shook his head. "He was only twelve when Mom kicked us out, and I had to work a couple of jobs just to keep a roof over our heads. I wasn't there for him like he needed, and he fell in with a bad crowd. Stupid me thought it was something he'd grow out of, but..."

His voice trailed off and it took all of Shelby's willpower not to pull him into her arms and tell him everything would be okay, even if it wasn't true. She held her breath and waited for him to continue.

"Shane was barely eighteen the day the cops raided our apartment. I was in law school at the time. I knew with the amount of heroin they confiscated, he'd be looking at ten years hard time, maybe more. They would've tried him as an adult too. I couldn't let that happen."

Her heart stuttered, stopped. Restarted again. "Are you telling me you confessed to keep your brother from going to jail?"

Chase gave a silent nod, and she couldn't resist snuggling closer into his side. That was the bravest, most selfless, most reckless thing she'd ever heard. Still, a man would be bitter about going to prison, no matter the circumstances. "I'm so sorry that happened to you, Chase, I really am. You didn't deserve that, but it still doesn't erase the fact that if my dad hadn't pointed them to your address, none of this would've happened."

"You don't know that. No one does. Hell, given the assholes Shane was hanging with and my fault for putting him there, your father is so far down on the list of people to blame he doesn't even register. No motive here, not from me. Besides, I had no idea it was your dad that tipped them off. He was a highly-regarded businessman, an honest guy."

Confession time. She straightened, withdrawing from the heat and strength of him to say what she had to say. "Maybe not so honest."

"Huh?" His confusion was written all over his face.

"My dad knew about the drugs running in and out of his casino. Had watched it go on for years. He even took a cut of the profits." She pushed a stray blond curl behind her ear with her free hand. "I'm guessing he told the cops about your brother to deflect heat away from him. Your brother was probably a small-time dealer, and Dad had way bigger investments to protect."

"Damn." This time, Chase leaned into her. "Well, it doesn't matter now."

She shrugged. "I feel bad for whoever takes over the Lucky Ace now that Dad's gone. They'll have a hell of a mess to clean up."

"Still, somebody will buy it. That's prime real estate right there."

"Maybe."

Chase smiled and bumped her shoulder with his, turning her tactics back on her. "Maybe. Is that all you have to say?"

"I guess." She smiled back. "How old were you when your mom kicked you out?"

"Nineteen. That's the only reason they let Shane stay with me instead of shipping him off to foster care. Legal age in Nevada is eighteen."

"Wow." She squeezed his hand again, feeling closer to him than anyone else in her life at the moment. "So, you've been alone since you were nineteen?"

"I've been alone since I could walk."

The rough edge to his voice broke her heart. "Not even a pet? Nothing?"

"Not even a pet." He flashed a rueful grin. "No time."

"Maybe you should get a pet of your own, since Henry's with Blake now. Animals like you. They know good people when they see them."

Chase laughed.

"I'm not kidding. A pet would help make your life less lonely. Believe me, I know."

He slipped a finger beneath her lowered chin and forced her to meet his gaze. "I know another way to be less lonely."

Her eyes slipped closed as his soft lips brushed over hers.

14

———

After leaving Blake's home later that afternoon, Shelby stopped by Paws and Play to check on the residents and let them out for a potty break and some play time. On her way toward the back area, she snagged a week's worth of accumulated mail off the receptionist's desk then set about opening cages and ushering several dogs out into the small fenced in area in the back of the building. She felt more buoyant and cheerful than she had in weeks.

An hour later, with all the food and water bowls refilled and everyone secured back in their pens, she sat at her work station in one corner and sorted through the assorted junk and bills. Most of it went in the trash or in her To-Be-Paid stack, but one letter had her halting. The federal seal of the United States covered one corner and beneath was a familiar address.

The grant application decision.

Nerves and adrenaline made her fingers shake as she ripped the top of the envelope open. These funds were a mainstay of her budget. Without a regular supply of grant money, non-profits like her shelter were dead in the water. They'd never denied her before, but considering all the other crazy events happening in her life right now, she wasn't certain of anything anymore....

Shelby closed her eyes and pulled out the letter, then squinted one eye open to read the first line. "Dear Ms. Bryant, we regret to inform you that your grant application for the next fiscal quarter has been denied..."

Her heart sank. No. They couldn't deny her application. She'd done everything right, filled out all the forms, written all the essays, dotted every I and crossed every T. Same as every other time when she'd been approved, no questions asked.

It made no sense. None whatsoever. Except...

Katherine. Has to be. But why would she sabotage my shelter?

The money. It was all about the money with her step-monster. Katherine would know that losing the grant money would make Shelby even more reliant on her dad's fortune to make ends meet and give her even more motive to kill her father..

Defeated, Shelby covered her face with her hands. Much as she hated to admit it, this time Katherine Bryant was right. If she wanted to save her shelter, she needed her dad's money after all.

15

Nine a.m. Monday morning found Chase back in the police interrogation room. Again. The only thing that had changed around this sorry place in the nearly forty-eight hours since he'd been there last was his attitude.

The black cloud of uncertainty that had hovered over him since he'd walked out of the prison dissipated, leaving in its wake a new determination, a new optimism. He could handle this, no matter what absurd accusation the cops came up with against him next. There was no way they could prove he had killed Warren Bryant no matter how many trumped up pieces of evidence Katherine gave them.

Calm and less stressed, he leaned back in his chair and clasped his hands atop his taut stomach, waiting for his favorite pain-in-the-butt detective to walk through the door.

He didn't have to wait long.

Detective Moore stalked in, her high-heeled pump clacking against the tiled floor and her expression impassive, as always.

Chase smiled. Good old Moore. Predictable to a fault. "We have to stop meeting like this."

She slid into the metal chair across the table from him, her cool half-grin not reaching her dark eyes. "Or you could just confess and make my life a lot easier."

"Sorry. No can do." He shrugged. "So, what do you think I did this time?"

"Kill Warren Bryant."

"Been there, didn't do it. Already told you that. Next."

"Right." Moore slid several photos across the table. "What about this heroin we found yesterday in a gym locker registered under your name?"

"Huh, really?" Chase glanced at the pictures. "Never seen those lockers before. And the only place I work out is the employee gym at Rockford Security. Sorry. Find my prints on the dope?"

"No, but we found your note to a rival dealer, telling them they'd better close up shop on your turf or else you'd give them the same treatment you gave Bryant."

"Dealer, eh?" Chase shook his head. The only dealer he knew these days was Shane—not that he'd tell that to the cops. "No dealers in my address book, Detective."

"Well, it's not like you'd flaunt that association all over town, would you, Mr. Evans?" Moore sat forward and flashed a full, smug grin at him now. From the confident set of her shoulders and the way she practically reeked of power, he guessed she had something more on him—or at least thought she did. "But..."

"But what?"

"We've got a guy in lock-up who says otherwise."

Disbelief made him chuckle. "What? Wait a second. You're telling me a drug dealer conveniently pointed the finger at me? I suppose you offered him a deal, right? Maybe even dropped my name?"

When Moore didn't respond, Chase sat forward. "I thought so. And you don't find that the teeniest bit suspicious?"

Moore sat back, eyes narrowed, silent.

"Mind telling me the name of this kingpin genius?"

"You know I can't divulge that information."

"Sure, okay." Certainty bubbled hot in Chase's gut.

"I'd say that's because you don't know. You guys got nothing on me. Nothing." He took a deep breath and forced a small smile. "And you know why, Detective? Because you're looking at the *wrong person*."

"Really?" Moore crossed her arms. "And where should we be looking, Mr. Evans? At your pretty little girlfriend?"

Definitely not the direction he'd meant to guide them. His sunny mood darkened. Trouble was, his current case against Katherine was just as circumstantial as theirs against him and Shelby. The whole thing was a catch twenty-two, a no-win scenario. He needed to find something substantial tying Katherine to her husband's murder, something more than tacky burner phones and missing envelopes of cash. Something real and true and irrefutable.

As Moore exited, leaving him alone again, his next move became clear.

He needed to sneak back into the Lucky Ace.

And this time he couldn't afford to get caught because he had the sickening feeling that the next time he set foot in this police station Moore and her minions would nail his ass to the wall for his supposed crimes and even Blake Rockford, with all impressive influence and favors, wouldn't save him from his fate.

THAT NIGHT, Chase stood outside Shelby's apartment door for the second time in a week and fidgeted while the sounds of Snickerdoodle's barking and Shelby's admonishments drifted to a halt. Shelby had mentioned over the phone that the big furry guy had finally gotten his cone removed, so he'd brought along a special surprise for the dog to celebrate.

Shelby opened the door and looked adorable as always in her baggy T-shirt and jeans. Her expression, however, appeared tragic and his heart ached at the sight. He stepped inside, closed the door behind him and offered Snickerdoodle one of the special hand-baked treats before shrugging out of his denim jacket. Concerned, he moved closer to Shelby and placed a hand on her shoulder. "What's wrong?"

"Katherine." Her voice quavered, but her tone spit venom. "Guess what I got in the mail yesterday? A great big denial on my latest non-profit grant."

"Shit. I'm sorry."

Shelby shook her head, her blond curls jiggling. "Not only that, but when I tried to order more food for the animals earlier, they declined my credit card. I called the company and found out my account's been cancelled. All my bank accounts are frozen, Chase. And no one will even tell me why."

Chase fisted his free hand, imagining it squeezing Katherine's neck instead. That woman was a goddamned menace to society. It was one thing for her to go after him, quite another for her to attack Shelby —the sweetest, kindest, most beautiful person he'd ever met.

"I-I'm going to lose the shelter, C-chase." Shelby hiccupped on her sobs. "Where will all my animals go? I'd keep them here, but I'm not sure I'll even have a home after all this is over."

"C'mere." Chase pulled her into his arms, holding her tight against his chest, offering her what comfort he could. He'd never really had a chance to be there for someone like this. Shane had always been closed off, even as a kid, refusing to confide in Chase about anything in his life after their mom had deserted them. It felt good and he wanted to be there for Shelby, wanted to honor the trust she'd put in him by making everything better for her.

Except he didn't know how. Not yet anyway.

They needed a plan—a worst case scenario modus operandi.

"Listen." He cupped her cheeks and forced her to

meet his gaze. Tears streamed down her flushed cheeks and her pretty blue eyes looked huge. He wanted nothing more than to kiss her and stroke her back and comfort her until she smiled again, but right now she needed more from him than physical caresses. She needed his emotional strength and support. "It'll be okay. I promise. If you have to close the shelter, we'll find homes for all the animals. They won't go back out on the streets. We'll keep them safe and protected, okay?"

She sniffled. "How? I have a lot of animals."

"And I know a lot of Rockfords."

Shelby snorted and swiped the back of her trembling hand beneath her eyes. "Katherine's behind this. I know it. We have to make her pay, Chase. She can't get away with this."

"We will." He leaned down, unable to resist giving her a quick kiss. "I promise."

Resolved, he took a seat on her sofa and pulled her down beside him. Snickerdoodle jumped up on the other end, searching around for more treats. He'd considered asking Shelby to come with him when he snuck back into the casino, but now, no way. If she got caught trespassing once more in Katherine's condo, chances were far higher she'd get charged too.

No. This was a mission he'd complete on his own.

Risky? Hell, yeah. But now he'd risk anything to keep Shelby safe.

Even his precious freedom.

———

SHELBY SNUGGLED CLOSER into Chase's side and rested her head against his shoulder. After her tear-filled meltdown, they'd decided to chill at her place and watch movies. She'd ordered a pizza and opened a bottle of chardonnay from her fridge, and they'd spent some nice quiet time together. It felt good—awesome, really—to be alone and relax with someone where she didn't have to be on guard or pretend to be someone or something she wasn't.

With Chase, she could just be herself and know that was okay, that was enough.

He kissed the top of her head and stroked his fingers through her hair, chuckling at the antics of the zany actors on screen. He'd sat through her favorite romantic comedy even though she was sure a tough guy like him would've preferred a blow-em-up action flick instead. His kindness made her care for him all the more. And those feelings seemed to be going around too, seeing as how one of her two hermit cats had jumped up and now rested across the back of the sofa behind Chase's head, his ginger tail swishing near Chase's ear.

Snickerdoodle, though, had claimed the prime real estate, draping himself across Chase's lap with his hind legs stretched atop Shelby's. The somewhat awkward arrangement still worked, since they used his long back as a table for their dinner plates. Shelby snickered while Chase slipped the dog tidbits of pepperoni from his meal. "You're a dog person aren't you?"

"I guess." Chase shrugged and grinned. "And you like cats?"

"I like both. And birds. And horses. And—"

"And every other creature on God's green earth, right?"

She laughed. "Yeah, pretty much. Not bugs though. Not a fan of those."

"What?" He looked at her with mock affront. "You got something against tarantulas?"

"Uh, yeah." The movie ended and she grabbed the remote. "What should we watch now? I picked the last time, so it's your choice."

"Hmm. Okay." He took the remote and scrolled through the onscreen choices, stopping at a newer release horror flick. "What about this one? Zombies too scary?"

"Nah. Zombies work for me."

"Cool." Chase started the new film then tossed the remote on the coffee table where their feet rested. Snickerdoodle grew restless and they both barely managed to pick up their plates before the dog jumped down. "Well, okay then. Guess he didn't appreciate being disturbed."

"Guess not." Shelby finished her last few bites of pizza then set her plate on top of the empty pizza box. "Oh well, his loss."

"Got that right." He waggled his eyebrows provocatively at Shelby. "I've been known to have the best lap in town."

She giggled. "I'll take your word for it."

"Your loss." He set his plate atop of hers on the table then pulled her tight into his side again, his hand resting comfortably at her waist. "Let me know if you change your mind."

As the film progressed and the scenes moved from infected hospital patients to a mass of drooling undead chomping on brains, Chase kept up a running commentary of funny remarks. Normally, people who talked constantly during movies got on Shelby's last nerve, but his humor made it fun.

"What do you think they make those brains out of?" Chase asked, his expression serious.

"No idea." Shelby shrugged. "Gelatin maybe?"

"Really? Gelatin? What flavor?"

"I don't know, brain flavor?"

"Okay, ew." He laughed. "Don't you ever think about stuff like that? Like people get paid excellent money for all these special effects things and I think that's fascinating. I watched a documentary once about how those guys make all that stuff and they said most of what they use are normal things you have in your kitchen. Like corn syrup and red food coloring for the blood and stuff."

Shelby leaned away and looked him in the eye. "Well, I can honestly say I've never, ever thought about blood flavored gelatin until tonight, Chase. Thanks for the new experience."

"I aim to please."

"I'm sure you do."

Snickerdoodle returned from the kitchen, his muzzle wet and dripping from the drink of water he'd obviously gotten and he eyed Chase's lap again. Chase patted his lap and Snickerdoodle jumped up and they all settled back in. Shelby drew a deep sigh of satisfaction, even though the day had been crappy, the evening was turning out absolutely perfect.

16

———

The next night, Chase hovered near the side employee entrance to the Lucky Ace, tension gnawing a hole in his gut. At least darkness had fallen about an hour earlier, giving him better cover for the covert nature of his mission. The alley adjacent to the door appeared empty too, making him feel a tad less apprehensive.

He leaned against the brick wall to wait for Owen. He'd texted the guy before leaving Blake's house and feigned a need to pick something up for work as an excuse to come to the casino. Dangerous, sure, but what other choice did he have? He needed dirt on Katherine Bryant and where better to find it than in her condo?

The metal door beside him pushed open and Owen Rockford peeked his head out, punctual as always. "Hey, man. Should you be here?"

"No," Chase said. "Definitely not. But like I said—"

"I know what you said." Owen blocked the entrance with his muscled bulk. "Now tell me why you're really here."

Well, shit. Chase exhaled and kicked a non-existent pebble with the toe of the black motorcycle boot. "C'mon, Owen. If I don't find something on Katherine, I could end up back in prison. And now Shelby's going to end up homeless. I can't let that happen, man."

Owen regarded him with a narrowed brown gaze for several seconds before stepping aside and cocking his head toward the casino interior. "Whatever. Fine. Get in here then."

They walked side by side down the back service halls toward the same entrance he'd gone out onto the casino floor with Shelby a few nights earlier. The one closest to the executive offices and the private elevator to Katherine's condo.

"You know if you get caught, I'll lose my job." Owen paused outside the door to the casino. "Please, man. For both our sakes, play it cool, eh?"

"Will do." Chase leaned a hip against the door to open it. "Cameras off?"

Owen backed away, hands up and head nodding. "I did not see you here tonight because I'm long overdue to leave."

Great. After a deep breath, Chase headed out into the marble hallway and over to the elevators, head down and baseball cap pulled low over his eyes. He'd just reached into his pocket for his trusty latex gloves when he collided hard with another person.

"Excuse me." Startled, he glanced up to find himself face-to-face with Katherine Bryant. *Crap.* The gleam of triumph in her eyes made his skin crawl.

She clucked her tongue, shaking her head as she crossed her arms. "Chase Evans. Never a smart move to return to the scene of your crime. Didn't they teach you anything in prison?"

Chase shoved the now useless gloves back into his pocket, his pulse thudding loud in his ears. He wouldn't give her the satisfaction of a response. He wouldn't.

"What's the matter, Chase?" Katherine tilted her head and wrinkled her nose. "Worried about your new little sex toy? Be a shame for Shelby to lose that shelter." Her tone reeked with insincerity. "Especially with her father dead. Accidents happen so easily these days, don't they?"

All his protective instincts blended with his

loathing for the bitch before him. Without considering his actions, Chase leaned close, his expression leaving no doubt that he meant business. The thought of anyone or anything hurting Shelby made him damned near homicidal. Katherine stepped back against the wall.

He lined in, jabbing a finger at her face. "I swear to God, you pathetic, conniving bitch. If you touch one hair on Shelby's head or harm her in any way, you'll pay. Understand?"

Katherine chuckled, not appearing the least bit concerned. "You never were the sharpest crayon in the box, were you, Chase? Guess dropping out of law school was a good career choice."

"Hey!" A security guard called from the other end of the hall. Chase's stomach nosedived to his toes. *Crap.* He'd played right into the bitch's hands. The guard pulled his Taser and pointed it directly at Chase. "Step away from the lady, sir, and put your hands behind your head."

Chase did, glancing over as another guard joined the first and moved closer to frisk him. Neither of the two were Rockford employees, unfortunately, meaning, there was no way in hell he could talk them out of another trip to police central. Especially once Katherine started her show.

Katherine stumbled forward, fake tears streaming down her cheeks as she grasped one of the guard's beefy bicep with her shaking hand. "Thank God you showed up when you did. This man is a known felon and I was terrified he'd kill me like he did my husband."

One guard placed a comforting arm around Katherine's shoulders and pulled her off to the side while the other secured Chase's wrists behind his back with a set of cuffs, then radioed in for the cops.

Yeah, it's going to be another long night.

IT WAS close to midnight before they finally released Chase from police custody. Thankfully, Moore had been out on another case, so at least he didn't have to spend his time playing Twenty Questions with her again. Still, his temples throbbed and his neck and upper back were stiff from stress, but at least he was a free man again.

At least for a little while longer anyway.

He stopped at the evidence window to collect his belongings, then headed out into the brightly lit LVPD station lobby. Like Vegas itself, the place went twenty-four-seven.

No rest for the wicked, as they say.

Head lowered, he walked over to where Blake sat near the far corner of the space. "Thanks for coming to get me, man. I still can't believe they dropped the charges. I figured after everything that's happened, they'd nail my ass to the wall this time." He looked away and cringed. "I can't believe I walked right into her trap. God, I'm such an idiot."

"Yeah. Not exactly a brilliant move there, genius," Blake said. "And they caught you on camera too, dumbass. Not smart at all."

Heat prickled up from beneath the collar of Chase's black T-shirt. "Sorry."

"You should be." Blake walked out of the station. Chase trailed behind him like a guilty puppy. "And for your information, I *did not* get the charges dropped. The most I could do was pay your bail to get you released into my custody."

"Shit." Chase halted at the side of Blake's navy sedan. "I don't have the money to pay you back right now, but you know I will. Someday. And you know I'm grateful."

"Grateful, huh?" Blake glared at him over the roof of the car, "Grateful would be not going to jail in the first place. That would be grateful." He exhaled loud.

"Besides. What was I supposed to do, Chase? Let you rot away in there?" Blake cursed under his breath and yanked the driver's side door open. "What the hell were you thinking, going back to the Lucky Ace tonight?"

Chase released his pent-up breath and climbed into the car. "I wasn't."

"Damn straight you weren't." After cranking the engine on and revving the motor, Blake sped out of the station lot and into the bustling late-night traffic. Uncomfortable silence descended over them like a shroud.

Minutes past as the tension between them grew thicker, became damned near palpable. Unable to take it anymore, Chase attempted conversation. "So, you saw the footage, huh?"

"Yeah, I saw it." They swerved around a corner and Blake focused straight ahead. "You know, while I was sitting around waiting for the judge to set your bail."

Cursing, Chase scrubbed his hands over his face. "Look, man. I'm sorry, okay? I know I disappointed you and I made Rockford Security look really bad, but what was I supposed to do?"

"Rockford Security?" Blake did look at him then and Chase wished to hell he hadn't, given his sour expression and the fact The Hurt was in full force. "You were not on a job for me tonight. I made that perfectly clear to the judge. So the only person you made look bad was yourself, buddy."

Got that right. Chase sighed and stared out the window again, silent.

They stopped at a red light and Blake exhaled loud then rolled his neck, his tone emerging a tad less arctic. "What did she say to provoke you?"

Chase shrugged, still staring at the neon glow of the Strip beyond. "What does it matter?"

Not like he'd spill any information about his new, deeper relationship with Shelby to Blake anyway. That would only make the guy think he'd been right all along and there weren't enough animals in the world to adopt as revenge for the kind of supreme I-told-you-so that would most certainly follow.

The light turned green and Blake accelerated. "In case you weren't aware, I have lip readers on staff. If you don't tell me, I'll find out easy enough anyway."

Well, crap.

Chase smoothed his hands down the legs of his dark jeans and tried to make his response as innocuous as possible. "She threatened Shelby, okay?"

"Huh." A slow, knowing grin spread over Blake's face.

Chase battled the urge to punch his boss's smug smile clean off. "Don't go there, man."

"Go where?" Blake gave him some serious side-eye as they screeched around yet another corner. "Like I care about your love life."

"Just don't, all right? I can't take anymore shit tonight." Chase sighed.

"Right." Blake chuckled. "You do seem a bit stressed."

"Really? Because being accused of murder, arrested for assault, having your girlfriend's life threatened and her dreams destroyed if I can't solve this goddamned mess isn't enough to put a guy a little on edge about."

Girlfriend? That was the second time he'd thought of Shelby as *his* that night. Funny, but the idea of a life, a future, with her didn't scare him the way commitments always had in the past.

Chase shifted in his seat. In fact, sharing a life with Shelby sounded pretty damned heavenly. Of course, they hadn't really discussed those things at all. And wouldn't either. Not until this whole black cloud of uncertainty was lifted. Then, maybe, they might have a chance at something real.

"You need proof that bad, huh?" Blake asked, breaking him out of his reverie.

"I'm willing to risk going back to prison. What do you think?"

They headed out of Las Vegas proper and into the desert night toward Summerlin as Blake's stiff posture relaxed a tad. "I have a few people between assignments. I'll have them go over the footage and see if we can't find something, anything. We've already got a team studying the hard drive from Warren's office computer for the surveillance footage from those office cameras. They haven't uncovered anything yet, though, so I'm assuming he has it stored on an encrypted private server somewhere. It's a long shot, but if we can locate that server and the footage, there's an excellent chance we'll know who killed Warren Bryant. Owen's promised to keep an eye out for anything suspicious too."

Chase clenched his jaw as warmth welled in his chest. It had been so long, too long, since anyone treated him with respect, with dignity, with kindness. The fact Shelby and Blake and his family did so on a daily basis touched him more than he could say. "Thanks, man. I really do appreciate the help."

"Hey, I owe you my life. It's the least I can do."

Chase opened his mouth to argue. What he'd done that day on that security job long ago he would have done no matter what. He sure hadn't done it to get favors for life and wanted to assure Blake that he didn't owe him anything, but Blake held his hand up stopping him before he could get any words out. "And I hate to see a person like Katherine Bryant think she can get away with framing someone for murder."

17

ate the following afternoon Chase stood once
more outside the employee entrance at the
Lucky Ace. No cloak and dagger this time, thank God.
This time he was here legitimately, because of a phone
call from Owen he'd received shortly before leaving
Rockford Security for the day.

Jittery with adrenaline, he shuffled from foot to
foot to keep himself from going nuts. What seemed
like a millennium later, but probably had only been a
few seconds, the door opened and Owen leaned out.

"You found something?" Chase struggled to keep
the excitement from his tone.

Owen waved him inside then led him to his office.
"Not just something, my man. I found what you need."

"Seriously?"

"Seriously." Owen took a seat behind the bank of flat screen monitors and clicked a few keys on the computer in front of him. "Take a look at this. Already backed up to Rockford's servers too."

Chase leaned in over Owen's shoulder and squinted at the black and white footage. "Where's this at? I don't recognize the background."

"The VIP bar. Warren didn't have cameras in there, but the cops ordered me to install one after your first encounter with Katherine. Guess they figured it might come in handy."

Onscreen, a man stood with his back to the camera. His hair was dark and his jacket had some kind of logo on the front breast pocket. Chase squinted. He'd seen that logo somewhere before, but for the life of him, couldn't place it at the moment. His mind was racing too bad.

"So what exactly am I looking at?"

Owen grinned. "Wait for it."

In the next frame, Katherine charged into the shot and argued with the man. He stormed off, his back still toward the camera. Katherine's expression looked furious and desperate as she stalked off too.

Chase rubbed his eyes. "Sorry, but I don't see how her fighting with some strange guy is going to help me."

"It's not done yet." Owen pointed at the monitor again. "Watch."

The footage switched to Katherine's condo. She stalked in, apparently still pissed from her encounter with the mystery man, and paced for a moment before heading into the bedroom. Even with the shitty camera angle, Chase could see the corner of an open safe in the background. The door of the safe blocked whatever it was that Katherine removed, but she stuffed the object beneath one arm, closed the safe, then walked back out into the living room.

Antsy now, Chase grew impatient. "Still not seeing the benefit here, Owen."

"Patience, grasshopper." Owen clicked several more keys, then sat back and clasped his hands behind his head. "Jeez, are you always like this? You're like a frigging roadrunner on crack, man. Settle down already."

Chase gave him a dirty look. "Excuse me for having my life on the line here."

"Chill, okay? And have a look at these." Owen pulled out a digital camera and scrolled through several pictures taken somewhere outside. "There's Katherine walking up the stairs to—"

"Shit! Is that Shelby's apartment?"

"Yep. And I'm not even going to ask how you know

that, my man."

Chase gave him a disgruntled look. "Just keep showing the pictures."

Owen snickered. "Fine, dude. Don't get your panties in a wad. Here's one where you can see what she took from that safe. Left it on Shelby's doorstep too."

"What is it?"

"Some kind of a pin or brooch." He set the camera aside and pulled a tissue wrapped bundle from his pocket. Inside was the object in question. A stork with its wings spread, loaded with diamonds and gems and tacky yellow gold. "Ugly as hell, if you ask me. But whatever. Katherine's upstairs with the police right now reporting it missing."

"Shit." Chase backed away, panic setting in. "And you think it's a good idea for us to have it?"

"Relax." Owen rewrapped the thing and shoved it back in his pocket. "The minute she and the cops are gone, I'll return it to her condo. That'll make her look stupid when I send one of the guards to make sure she's okay." He winked and clasped his hands over his flat stomach. "I've been doing that, you know—interrupting her about once an hour—since she put you back in jail."

Chase paced the floor of the tiny room to burn off

some excess energy. "Still don't see how this will help. At most, all that missing brooch proves is she's trying to commit insurance fraud."

Owen gave him an impassive stare. "Were you always such an idiot or did prison rot your brain? This pin proves she's setting Shelby up. Coupled with the circumstantial video footage we have backed up that Katherine thinks she erased? It's enough to cast doubt on her accusations against you, man."

Chase froze. Maybe Owen was right. Maybe it would be enough for a jury's reasonable doubt. And maybe, if all that was true, then maybe, just maybe this whole thing would be over soon.

LATER, Chase returned to Shelby's apartment. He'd made up some excuse to Blake about spending time in the Rockford IT archives looking for more clues all night or something. Didn't really matter what he said. From the knowing look on Blake's face, he saw straight through Chase's lame excuse anyway.

He knocked on the door and laughed when Snickerdoodle bounded out to tackle him against the railing again. This was fast becoming a tradition between them and one he wouldn't mind continuing for a good long time. He held out yet another bag of homemade treats he'd picked up on the way over and Shelby took it, then scrunched her nose.

"What kind are these?"

"Not sure," Chase said, between doggy kisses. "Liver, I think is what the guy said."

"Huh." She sniffed them once more then held them at arm's length. "They smell like dirty feet."

"Nice." He pushed the slobbering, excited mutt off and walked inside, closing the door behind him. "Well, I guess it could be worse. I guess they could smell like—"

"And on that note." Shelby cut him off by kissing him long and deep. "I missed you."

"I missed you too." He squeezed her tight and smiled. "How was your day?"

"Okay. I got a few new residents in at the shelter." She pointed at a couple of new kitties joining the two already convalescing in her apartment. "They both have some anxiety issues, so I didn't want to leave them alone all night."

"Good move, crazy cat lady." Chase laughed and Shelby swatted him hard on the arm. Things felt so good when he was with her, natural and fun and not forced at all. Not like with other people. With others, he always felt like he had to be on his best behavior, like he was under constant scrutiny and constant pressure to surpass other people's expectations of how an ex-con should act, to prove himself worthy again. With Shelby, he could just be himself.

He took off his jean jacket and plopped down on the sofa. "I had an interesting meeting earlier with Owen Rockford."

"Yeah?" She sat next to him and snuggled into his side as he put his arm around her shoulders. "Anything useful about my step-monster?"

"Actually, yeah."

"Really?"

"Owen found some video footage of Katherine fighting with some guy down in the VIP bar, then going upstairs to pull something out of the safe. Turned out to be a brooch that she..." He hesitated. Part of him didn't want to hurt Shelby any more than she already had been, but the other part—the lawyer part—knew full disclosure was best. "Well, she tried to plant it here, outside your place, then report it stolen to the cops."

Shelby stiffened beside him, but didn't say a word.

He rubbed lazy circles on the soft skin of her shoulder where the neckline of her oversized T-shirt had slipped down. "Anyway, Owen saw what was going on and retrieved it before she ever called the cops. He said once the police finished interviewing her, he'd stow it back in her condo and make her look like a lying ass in front of the cops." Chase snorted. "There goes her credibility."

"Just like that, huh?" Shelby's voice wobbled a little, and Chase tucked her in tighter. "Wow."

"Yeah, just like that." He tipped her chin up with his finger. "You okay?"

Tears filled her pretty blue eyes. "I'm good. It's just a lot, you know?" She sniffled and lowered her head. "First my dad's death, then all this craziness. I never thought it would get this bad."

"Did something else happen today?" Concerned, he threaded his fingers through her silky blonde curls and savored the weight of her head on his chest. "You can tell me anything."

"I just... I don't know. You'll think I'm stupid."

"No, I won't." She raised her head and squinted at him. He gave her the time-honored Boy Scout sign. "Swear."

She sighed and leaned against him once more. "When my dad first started dating Katherine, I thought maybe things would finally work out for all of us. She seemed to genuinely love him and he was so happy when he was with her. I hadn't seen him that happy since my mom was alive." She rubbed her hand under her nose and gave a sad little chuckle. "I guess maybe I didn't want to see the signs. Signs that Katherine didn't really care as much about him as she did his fortune. It's all so heartbreaking, when you think about it." Her shoulders shook and Chase cupped her cheek, pulling her tighter into his chest. "M-my daddy's gone. I l-loved him so much and now h-he's gone and I'm all alone a-and…"

Shelby's sobs ripped his heart to pieces. He kissed the top of her head, inhaling the scent of her floral shampoo and closed his eyes. He'd stay here forever if he could, or as long as she'd have him. "You're not alone. Not anymore."

She sniffled and looked up at him. "I'm not?"

"Nah." He grinned. "You can't scare me away that easily."

"Oh." She placed her palm against his chest and sat up, the heat of her touch burning all the way through to his soul. Even with flushed cheeks and a red nose from crying, she was the most beautiful thing he'd ever seen. Shelby wiped her eyes. "I'm sure I look like a complete mess. Sorry. I didn't mean to get so emotional about everything. And I'm overjoyed to hear about the footage on Katherine."

"Good to know. Next time I see you bawl I'll know that's what you do when you're happy." His effort to lighten the somber mood between them earned him a punch to the arm. "What?"

"I don't make a habit of crying on men's shoulders."

"Also good to know."

"I just..." She shrugged. "I just feel really comfortable around you, I guess."

Chase smiled slowly and took her hand. "You do, huh?"

"Yeah. I do." She tucked a stray curl behind her ear. "Which is good, after all the stuff that happened with us."

"Hmm." He laced their fingers together. "Hey, um, speaking of that, I wondered if maybe...if, uh..." Chase frowned and turned away. "Dammit, my words are getting all tangled."

This time, Shelby laughed. "Really? I'll alert the press. Talkative Chase Evans is tongue tied."

"No, seriously. You get me all flustered."

"I do?" The pretty pink color in her cheeks heightened, and he couldn't resist stroking his finger over the smooth flesh.

"Yeah, you do." Chase looked deep into her sparkling blue eyes, putting all his emotions on the line. "What I wanted to ask was after all this is over, do you think that maybe, possibly..."

"Spit it out."

"Would you consider being my girlfriend?" There. He'd said it. Ball in her court now.

Her brows rose. "Girlfriend? Like dates and dinners and sharing stuff?"

"Uh, yeah. Even the crazy Sunday get-togethers with the Rockfords, if you're game."

"Wow." She frowned and for a pulse-stopping second he feared he was in for the big rejection. Then she gave him her sweetest smile, the one that electrified his whole body and made his battered heart rejoice. "I think maybe we could work that out."

He inched closer, his heartbeat pounding. "So, that's a yes?"

She met him halfway, her lips mere millimeters from his. "A most definite maybe."

"I'll take it." He captured her mouth with his before she could say another word.

All his life he'd searched for one safe place. One secure place. One place to call home.

He'd never dreamed he'd find all three in Shelby's arms. As he kissed her, he knew deep inside he'd do anything to protect the woman he loved.

Loved?

Yeah, he loved Shelby.

Even if he couldn't say the words yet.

18

———

B*uzz. Buzz. Buzz.*

Chase squinted an eye open into the darkness and for a moment wondered where in the hell he was. There was something soft and warm pressed against his side and a hard lump covering his feet. Normally, when he jolted awake in the middle of the night, fears bombarded him and he imagined himself back in prison.

Except this time was different.

The sweet smell of flowers coaxed him to burrow deeper beneath the covers once more. Shelby. He was with Shelby, in her apartment.

From the end of the bed, Snickerdoodle snored louder than any human he'd ever known and Chase couldn't help but grin. For the first time in memory, he was happy. Truly, deeply, wonderfully happy.

Buzzzzzz.

Shit.

He rubbed his eyes and glanced at the nightstand where he'd stashed his phone. Maybe if he ignored whoever it was, they'd go away. Calls in the middle of the night were never a good omen anyway, right? The phone stopped ringing and silence filled the small studio apartment once more. Chase snuggled down beside Shelby and closed his eyes.

Buzz. Buzz. Buzz.

Crap.

Immensely irritated, he pushed up onto his elbows and reached over for the damned device. Whoever was on the other end of the line better have said their prayers, 'cause they'd be dead soon.

Shelby stirred and looked over her shoulder at him, groggy. "What's going on?"

"Nothing." The screen flashed Blake's name. *Shit.*

Considering he was either in for another ass-reaming because his boss had discovered he'd lied about his whereabouts or they'd discovered something new about the murder case, he figured upright and alone was the best way to have this conversation.

He threw his legs over the side of the bed and stood. "I have to take a call. Go back to sleep."

He tugged on his jeans then kissed her softly before heading out the front door to the small landing beyond. The phone rang for the fourth time and he growled as he hit the Answer button. "This better be good."

"Where the hell are you?" Blake's irritation rippled through the phone line.

"I'm..." He ran a hand through his bed-head hair. Lying to Blake after all he'd done didn't sit right, but he sure wasn't about to let the guy know his actual location. Not yet anyway. Things with Shelby were still too new, too fresh, too precious. "I'm fine. What's going on?"

"We found the footage from Warren's office on the day of the murder."

"What?" Adrenaline shocked him fully awake. "That's awesome."

"Actually, no. It's not." Blake's serious tone settled in Chase's chest like a boulder. "You're not going to like it."

"Why not?"

"This isn't something you want to hear over the phone. Trust me." Blake sighed. "Come into the office."

The Rockford offices were where he was supposed to be already. The fact Blake knew he'd lied about his whereabouts, yet didn't berate him for it, troubled him even more. Blake always gave him a hard time about stuff like that. *Well, shit.* "Uh, yeah, okay."

"I know you're at Shelby's, Chase."

"Look, man. I'm sorry I lied, but—"

"Save it." Blake sounded thoroughly exasperated. "Why didn't you just bring her to the house?"

"She has pets."

"So do I, now, thanks to you. What? Would they eat Henry or something?"

He thought about Snickerdoodle's banana-pants reaction to those dumbass liver treats and thought, yeah maybe he would—if the lizard was slathered in liver pate. "I don't know."

"Look, whatever. Just get your ass into the office. I've already sent a car to pick you up. Should be pulling up to the curb as we speak."

Sure enough, he looked down to see a gray sedan now idling in the complex's parking lot. "Fine. I'll be right there."

Chase ended the call and slipped back into the apartment, dressing as quickly and quietly as possible to avoid waking Shelby. He pulled on his boots and grabbed his jacket then tiptoed over to kiss her one last time on the forehead. Snickerdoodle whined from the end of the bed, and Chase gave the mutt a quick scratch behind the ears. "I wish I could stay here too buddy. Believe me."

Cool desert air brushed his face as he stepped outside and headed down the creaking metal stairs to the company car. Before he reached his ride, however, a figure stepped from the shadows.

Dark hair, expensive clothes, piss-poor attitude.

Katherine.

Could this night get any worse?

Beneath the orange streetlights, she thrust something in front of his face. Something glittery and gaudy as hell.

The brooch.

Apparently, yes. This night could get much, much worse.

"If you knew about this, then you know I tried to stash it at your girlfriend's. *Someone* messed with my plan." Her voice seethed with venom. She stashed the pin away and instead pulled out her cell phone. "I'm sick of you poking your nose in where it doesn't belong. You're nothing but a worthless felon, bad DNA through and through, and yet you think you're good enough to mess with me. Well, you're not. And this just proves my point."

She shoved the phone in his face next, the small screen filled with the now familiar black and white security footage from the Lucky Ace. Chase recognized the interior of Warren Bryant's office and his throat constricted as he watched a very much alive Warren working at his desk. The man went through files, signed documents, took a drink from a glass near his side.

Moments later, he slumped over his desk, apparently asleep. Or worse.

Bile rose and Chase swallowed hard to ease the burning. A man entered from screen left and rounded the desk to stand beside Bryant. The guy looked straight into the security camera.

Chase's world teetered before plunging off a sharp, endless precipice.

No. It couldn't be. He couldn't believe it. Wouldn't believe it.

You're not going to like it...

Blake's words mocked him, running an endless loop through his head. This must've been the video he'd wanted Chase to see.

Shane.

His own little brother. A murderer.

Inside, he screamed. Outside, he couldn't look away from the video, like a train wreck happening right before his eyes. Onscreen, Shane pulled a syringe from the pocket of his black coat—one of the same embroidered designer jackets he'd seen that day in the apartment—and plunged the needle into the side of Warren Bryant's neck. Within seconds, Bryant's body went into convulsions, most likely from an overdose. Chase was surprised the rational part of his brain still functioned enough to supply that detail about the drugs because the rest of him sure as hell wasn't functioning on all cylinders.

Onscreen, Shane shoved the now empty syringe back into his pocket then set something onto Bryant's desk before exiting. Katherine enlarged the picture to focus on the object left behind.

My letter opener. My commendation letter opener.

Chase's heated blood froze to ice. Now he knew what really happened to it. Shane hadn't pawned it for money, like he'd led Chase to believe that day in his apartment. No. He'd used it to let Chase take the fall. Again.

Moore's words came back to him. She'd said they had proof he was in Bryant's office. She must have been talking about the letter opener and it probably had his fingerprints all over it.

Pain and betrayal, worse than he'd ever experienced before—not when their dad left, not when their mom kicked them out, not even when Shane let him take the responsibility for his drug wrap—seared his insides, eating up what joy he had left.

"See." Katherine shoved the phone back in her coat pocket, her smile smug. "There you go. Your own pathetic kin couldn't even care less about you. All of you Evans boys are nothing but worthless trash. Less than worthless. Purely expendable, really."

Chase forced words past his tight vocal cords. "That's why you pinned this on me?"

"Of course."

"But how could either of you know I'd even get the job at the casino?"

Katherine shrugged. "Educated guess. With your past conviction, and your ties to Blake Rockford—which your brother so eagerly provided, by the way—it made sense. All I had to do was request a bodyguard and boom, there you were. Only thing I didn't expect was for you to run out that first night. Figured a hard-up ex-con like you would pounce on the first woman who offered him nookie. I'd planned to keep you in my bed until after the murder, but you went and screwed up that plan." She tossed her long brown hair over her shoulder and studied her perfectly mani-cured nails. "Oh well. It all still worked out in the end, didn't it?"

Her smiled was cold enough to freeze ice.

"You won't get away with this." Chase clenched his hands at his sides to keep from choking her.

"Already did, thanks." She looked up at him and batted her heavily-mascaraed eyes. "See, this is how things will go down. You'll confess to Warren's murder and you'll say you did it for your whore of a girlfriend up there, or else I'll give this video to the cops."

"I won't implicate Shelby in this mess."

"No?" Katherine snorted. "Not even to save your beloved little brother? He's the only family you've got now, Chase, sad excuse for a man that he is. You were his hero five years ago. He told me so."

A choice he'd never, ever wanted to make.

The woman he loved or the brother he'd sworn to protect.

A choice he couldn't make.

"No. I'll confess, but I won't tie anyone else to the crime. Take it or leave it."

Katherine frowned. "Dammit. You are a stubborn, noble thing, aren't you? Fine. Whatever. I don't care how you confess, only that you do. It won't be as convenient for me, money-wise, but I'll deal."

"Deal how?"

"Don't worry, Chase." She backed into the shadows once more. "I always have a plan."

Numb, he stumbled to the car and climbed into the passenger seat. He didn't recognize the guy driving, but it was just as well. With his mind spinning a billion miles an hour, he couldn't really talk anyway.

The future. The hopes he'd had. The dreams.

Gone. All gone. With one choice. A choice he had no option but to make.

No more freedom. No more family. No more Shelby.

The IT room at Rockford Security buzzed with activity when Chase walked in half an hour later. He spotted Blake near the far corner of the room and headed over. The shock from his encounter with Katherine had worn off, leaving in its wake exhaustion and resignation.

These would be his last few hours as a free man. He should be out enjoying them, not stuck in some dreary computer lab. But Blake had put himself on the line more times than Chase could count over the past couple of weeks and damn if he'd let the guy down again.

"Hey." He walked up to the cubicle where Blake stood, hunched over the shoulder of one of the techs, pointing at something onscreen. He did his best to school his features into bland indifference, but if the concern in Blake's eyes was any indication, he'd failed. "I'm here."

"I see that." With a sharp order, Blake cleared the room, leaving the two of them alone in the department. The air hummed with the whirr of machines and the stench of regret. Blake waited until the door closed behind the last tech, then hung his head. "I'm sorry about this, Chase. Really I am."

He played the footage. The same footage Chase had witnessed on Katherine's phone—same syringe, same scenario, same betrayal. He'd figured seeing it a second time would've lessened the impact, but it still hit like a sucker punch to the solar plexus.

The video onscreen ran its course then went to fuzz.

Chase squeezed his eyes shut and looked away.

Blake clicked a few keys then faced Chase once more. "I expected more of a reaction."

Chase shook his head and stared at the bland beige wall across from him.

"You knew, didn't you?" Blake scowled, arms crossed. "For how long?"

After a deep breath, Chase answered. "Not long. About a half hour." He scrubbed a hand over his face, like that might erase the memory of a gloating Katherine. "Found out just after you called."

He felt the weight of Blake's stare on him even though he didn't look at him. "I'm going over to the police station in the morning and confessing. After I say goodbye to Shelby."

"Confessing?" Blake sounded flabbergasted. "Why?"

"C'mon, man. I can't let Shane go to prison. He'd never survive and I owe him. After everything we went through, I owe him big time. It was my fault. All of it. So I'll do this for him, not because I'm guilty, but because it's the right thing to do, okay?" He faced his boss and held up a hand when Blake tried to interrupt. "Don't. Just don't. Don't tell me you wouldn't do exactly the same thing for any one of your siblings, because I know you would. In a heartbeat."

Blake closed his mouth.

"Yep. That's right." Chase cursed and turned away. "You do for family. Period."

A few moments later, Blake finally spoke. "That's what happened last time too, isn't it?"

There was no longer a point in concealing the truth. "Yeah, it was."

"I thought so."

"You did?" Given Blake's nearly preternatural

instincts where people were concerned, Chase supposed he shouldn't have been surprised. "Yeah, you probably did. Listen, thanks for giving me the job when I got out and taking me under your wing and into your family. You all really helped me when I needed it, and I'll never forget your generosity."

"Don't do this, Chase. Please." Blake stepped toward him.

"I have to, man. You know that." Blinking hard, he started for the door. "I gotta go."

"Do you love her?" Blake called from behind him.

That stopped Chase in his tracks. "I do."

"Then maybe you should fight for her. Fight for that life."

Resigned, Chase hunched his shoulders and continued toward the exit. "Family first."

"Shelby could be your family too." Blake's words echoed through the empty office space, mirroring what Chase had thought too—before his universe imploded. "If you let her."

There was no car waiting this time when Chase stepped out into the chilly late-October night. Buses didn't run in the area at that hour either, so he walked in the direction of Shelby's apartment, several miles away. The exercise would do him good anyway, give him time to think, time to come up with a plan to implicate Katherine and make sure she did time for her crimes as well.

———

A KNOCK at the door awoke Shelby and she squinted into the pre-dawn darkness. She'd fallen back to sleep after Chase had gone outside for his phone call and now felt completely disoriented. The bedside clock showed four a.m. Had it really been that long since Chase had left her side? Was he locked out? Had he been pounding on the door this whole time?

Snickerdoodle whimpered from near her feet and she got out of bed, throwing on an old robe before padding across the room. Through the peephole, she gazed out to see Chase on the landing.

With one foot holding back the dog, she opened the door. "Have you been out there this whole time?" She rubbed her eyes with her free hand. He was fully dressed and the look on his face was awful. Something was wrong. Very, very wrong. Shelby stepped aside to let him in, her heart in her throat. "What's happened?"

"I was at the Rockford offices."

"You were?" Nose scrunched, she flipped on the lights then headed into the kitchen to start a pot of coffee. "I didn't even know you'd gone. I thought you locked yourself out when you took that phone call."

Chase waited until she pushed the Start button on the coffeemaker, then came up behind her. He didn't touch her, just stood there, with his hands in his pockets and his expression somber. "They found the footage from your father's office. From the night of his murder."

"Oh." Hands trembling, she gripped the edge of the counter. She'd always known this moment would come, she just didn't expect it to happen so soon, or so early in the morning. An odd mix of elation and dread filled her stomach. Whatever had been on those tapes must not have been good, if Chase's demeanor was any indication. "Who was it?"

Jaw tight, Chase stared at the floor, his words terse. "My brother, Shane."

"What?" All the air rushed from her lungs and Shelby's head spun. She reached for him, but he flinched away. "Oh, Chase. I'm so sorry. I—"

"Stop, please." He raised a hand and inhaled sharply. "I came to tell you myself, before... Well, before everything happens."

The finality of his tone sent a shiver of fear through her. "Before what happens?"

"I'm going to the police station from here to turn myself in."

"B-but you didn't do it." Her words sounded as jumbled as she felt. "Why would you do that, Chase? Why?"

"It doesn't matter if I did it or not, Shelby. If I don't confess, Katherine will give her copy of the footage to the police. I can't let that happen to Shane. He'd never survive prison. I would. I have. I will again."

Horror prevailed as the full ramifications became clear in her mind and her old insecurities resurfaced. Of course he'd leave her so easily. Abandon everything they had together. Why not? Everyone did. No one truly wanted Shelby Bryant around. She'd been a fool to think this gorgeous, brave, honorable man would be any different. Outrage flared hot and bright inside her. No. She might not be rich or beautiful or popular, but she was worth something, dammit. Worth the world to her animals and her shelter, and to Chase once too. He'd taught her that, if nothing else. Posture stiff and chest aching, she clutched the front of her robe closed like a shield. "So you're choosing your brother over me."

"Goddammit, Shelby. It's not like that. You're an only child. You wouldn't understand."

The coffeemaker beeped loud like a clarion call.

"Maybe I don't have brothers and sisters, but I do have common sense, Chase. You think your brother will learn something from this new sacrifice of yours? He won't. He obviously didn't after the first time you went away for his crimes. You can't keep doing for people and expect things to be different. I learned that the hard way and it looks like you need to as well. He'll never stop, Chase. Never stop taking advantage of you. He will never take responsibility for his life or his actions until he's forced to. Why can't you see that?" This time, she grabbed his arm before he could move away. Stepped closer and put her arms around his waist, pulling his tense form closer. "Please don't do this. Please."

He removed her hands and walked into the living room, increasing the distance between them. "Don't make this harder than it already is, Shelby. I've made my decision."

Anger and panic clogged her throat despite her resolve to stay calm. "Dammit, Chase, I thought we had something special. I-I thought—"

"We do." His voice sounded gruff and low. "We did."

"Then why, Chase? Why?" She bit back a sob, refusing to let him see her tears. Not this time. Not this way. "Why won't you stay with me?"

"I can't. I'm sorry. I wish more than anything in this world I could stay here with you forever, but I can't. I owe Shane. Owe him more than I can ever repay. But maybe sacrificing my happiness and future is a start."

Shelby shook with the effort to suppress her angry tears and turned away.

"Please, baby. Don't cry. Please…"

She heard the weight of his footsteps across the tiled floor then the warmth of his hand on her shoulder. It was the endearment, though, that was too much to bear. Inconsolable now, she wrenched free and into the corner of her tiny kitchen. "Don't touch me. Go. Just go and leave me alone."

Eyes squeezed shut, she waited—waited for the door to close behind him, for life as she knew it to end. Instead, she heard the rustle of plastic and her dog's satisfied woof.

"Here you go, boy," Chase said, followed by the chomp of Snickerdoodle eating something solid. "Enjoy."

Several more seconds passed, but Shelby refused to turn around, refused to look at him, refused to let him see just how much destruction his leaving caused her poor, scarred heart.

At last, she heard the door open amidst Snickerdoodle's high, lonesome whine. "Goodbye, boy. You be good for your mama now, okay?"

The sounds of distant traffic drifted in along with the cool night breeze. Then, just as suddenly as Chase Evans had entered Shelby's life, he was gone. The door clicked shut behind him with the resounding finality of cancer.

Legs shaking and pulse pounding, Shelby slid down the cabinets to the kitchen floor, her head in her hands and her tears now flowing freely. Snickerdoodle padded over to her and nuzzled her temple while she hugged him tight.

The dog was her only comfort now, her only friend.

Same as always.

20

By the time Chase arrived outside the Las Vegas Police Department headquarters, it was just after sunrise. The sky above was streaked with bright pinks and golds, and he did his best to savor every second, knowing this would be the last time in a long time he'd have the freedom to enjoy it.

Breaking up with Shelby had been the hardest thing he'd ever done in his life. Harder than raising Shane on his own, harder than standing trial for a crime he didn't commit, harder than going back to prison.

Back to prison.

The words didn't bother him as much now as he thought it would. Hell, at least he knew what to expect this time around, how to act, who to associate himself with for the maximum benefit. Head down, he took a deep breath and stalked toward the entrance to the station, his heart heavy and his pace determined.

Within two steps, he collided hard with another body.

"You're an idiot."

Liv? What the hell?

Stunned, Chase looked up to see Blake's sister glaring at him. Apparently, the guy had called out the reinforcements. Wouldn't work, though. He'd made up his mind and nothing would change it now. He tried to step around her, but she blocked his path again.

"No." She jabbed her finger hard into his chest, her tone hard as diamond. "You're going to listen to what I have to say, Chase Evans."

"Can't. Sorry. Places to go, people to see." He moved to the side again, but she blocked him. Exhaling, he shook his head. "Look, I get what your brother's trying to do here, but it's too late, okay? It's decided. It's none of his business anyway. Or yours. I don't work for you anymore. I quit."

"Doesn't matter."

"Obviously."

Hands on hips, she glanced around then lowered

her voice as several officers arrived for duty. "Listen to me, Chase. Don't do this. Don't confess."

Again with the guilt trip. He pinched the bridge of his nose between his thumb and forefinger. Did none of these people understand loyalty? He prayed for patience and walked on ahead despite her blocking his path. "I have to. He's my brother."

"Well, he's a damned shitty one. Always has been." She kept pace beside him.

"That's my fault too."

"How, Chase? How in the world could that possibly be your fault, huh?" She cut him off again. "Shane's an adult now. At some point his behavior stops being your fault and starts being his responsibility. You weren't his parent. Hell, you were barely an adult yourself when you had to take over raising him. You did the best you could. He's the one who decided the law didn't apply to him."

Chase forced his tense shoulder to relax. "You don't understand. I should've—"

"Should've what? You've already given up five years of your life for him, Chase. Don't make the same mistake twice. Besides, you both came from the same home, the same environment and you didn't turn out to be some drug-dealing killer."

He stared off into the horizon, where the sky shifted from pastel shades to bright blue, Katherine's bitter words slicing through what little self-respect he had left.

All of you Evans boys are nothing but worthless trash. Less than worthless. Purely expendable, really...

"I was lucky. I had Blake and you guys to help stabilize me. Shane didn't."

"And that's my point." Liv threw up her hands. "*We're* your family now, Chase. All of us Rockfords. Your true family, connected at the heart. Shane's only connected by blood."

He wanted to believe that more than he wanted anything in the world, except maybe Shelby. The wounds on his tortured soul bled anew. What he wouldn't give to hold her again, comfort her again, love her and make her his own. But that was all a dream now, had to be.

Chase side-stepped around Liv and stepped up onto the curb in front of the station. Shane might only be his family now by blood, but he was still family. "Look, I appreciate everything you all have done and for you being here today."

"Really? Then how about showing that appreciation."

"How?"

"By getting your ass back to Blake's house, by continuing on with your life. By waking up tomorrow morning and going to work like normal people."

"But Shane—"

"What about Shane?" Color flushed her cheeks and Liv's green eyes sparked with indignant fire. "If you quit treating him with kid gloves, maybe Shane would finally learn that the world doesn't revolve around him and that there are consequences for his actions. At this point, I bet he'd even flip on Katherine and get a reduced sentence for doing it, since he's a first-time offender." Her expression betrayed a hint of disgust. "He's obviously not averse to switching sides. Did that where you're concerned easily enough."

Despite the truth of her statement, Chase lashed out, hurt. "And what if he gets killed in prison? What then?"

"You did fine. What makes you think he'll do any worse?"

"Because."

"Because what? Because he's your little brother? Because you still think of him as a child when he's clearly an adult?"

Chase looked away, embarrassed and furious that her words hit far too close to home.

"That's right. Shane isn't stupid, Chase. In fact,

given the crowd he hangs with these days, I'd say he's far more savvy than you. He won't go looking for fights. And if he keeps his head down and finally learns to play by the rules, then he might even be eligible for early parole. Prison might just be the best thing that could ever happen to Shane Evans. Ever think of that?"

No, he hadn't, but maybe Liv was right.

He opened his mouth to respond, but she held up a hand.

"No. Save the excuses. You know as well as I do if you go back to prison, it won't just be for a couple of years this time. The prosecution will go for the jugular. A life sentence. Are you willing to throw away your new life? Shelby won't wait forever." She laid her hand on his forearm, the same as Shelby had done earlier. "You deserve a future, Chase. You deserve love. And God knows it's hard enough to find someone who wants to be with you and who you want to be with in return."

The yearning in her voice raised the ache in his heart to new levels. "You sound like you're speaking from experience."

She shrugged and stared at the brick wall of the station. "Maybe I am, maybe not. Either way. Please think about this before you go in there. Once you confess, there's nothing anyone can do to help you."

Chase took a deep breath and gave her a quick hug before stepping away, his mind whirling. "I'm good, Liv. Really. Thanks again for talking to me."

The automatic doors to the station swished open behind him and he gave her a final wave before stepping inside the brightly lit lobby. He stopped at the reception desk and asked for Detective Moore, stating he had new information about the Bryant murder. Moments later, he was escorted back to the same interrogation room he'd been in before to wait.

Moore entered a short time later. She flashed him a cold, polite smile as she took the seat across from him. "Mr. Evans, glad to see you this morning. Finally ready to confess, huh?"

He stared at her, all the conflicting ideas bombarding his exhausted brain. Katherine's threats against Shelby. What could happen to Shane in prison. All he'd give up by confessing to a second crime he didn't commit. Liv's statement about Shane needing to grow up, to take responsibility for his actions.

Chase pressed the heels of his hands hard against his eyes and inhaled.

It was time. Time for the truth. Time for answers. Time for justice to be done.

At last, he met Detective Moore's gaze direct, his calm voice at odds with the nervous fireworks bursting inside him. "I didn't kill Warren Bryant. But I know who did."

<hr>

A FEW HOURS LATER, Chase stood off to the side of the lobby while two officers led Shane Evans into the police station in handcuffs. He met his brother's harsh glare and did his best to convey his deep remorse that things had to turn out the way they did.

Shane wasn't having it, apparently. Instead he spat on the floor near Chase's feet as the officers tugged him past, his tone harsh with betrayal. "Judas. You're nothing but a fucking Judas and a lousy ass excuse for a brother."

Guilt and nausea roiled in Chase's stomach. He sucked in a breath to keep from puking. This was how it had to be, no matter how difficult. He knew that. Too bad the knowing didn't make the doing any easier. He forced his tense shoulders to relax and glanced at Detective Troy Atkins, who stood beside him. "Can I have a minute alone with him?"

"Sorry," Troy said. "That's not really allowed."

"C'mon, man. He's my flesh and blood. Please? I promise I won't say anything I'm not supposed to. You can listen in, if you want, to make sure. I just…" He glanced at the door through which they'd led Shane, heard his brother's hateful words echo inside his head like exploding grenades. "I need to make sure he knows how serious this is. Why I did what I did. Maybe I could convince him to cooperate."

Troy shook his head then looked at his watch. "Like I said, this isn't protocol. And I *will* be watching through the two-way mirror. One wrong word and it's my ass on the line, not just yours. Got it?"

"Got it." Chase followed the detective down the now familiar hallway. His chest squeezed tight with adrenaline.

"Five minutes." Troy walked to another door a few feet away. "Make them good."

Chase nodded, the metal handle of the door ice cold against his palm. He could do this. He would do this. Shane needed to know, needed to understand, needed to save himself as much as possible. He walked in to find Shane sitting in the seat Detective Moore had usually occupied during Chase questioning.

His brother looked up at him, his gaze as hard as

his expression. "You did this. You turned on me. Your own brother."

"Shit, Shane. You killed a man!" Chase ran a hand through his hair, agitated. "I don't give a damn why you did it—if Katherine Bryant had you wrapped around her finger with sex or drugs or money or whatever. You *murdered* someone, Shane." He punched the cement wall with his fist, craving the pain. "Then you set *me* up for it. After everything I did. After I gave you a second chance."

"Second chance?" Shane gave a derisive snort. "What does that even mean? A second chance for what? For the same old shitty life that I had before you went to prison? The same shitty life I've got now. Some second chance. Thanks, bro. Thanks a lot."

"I served five years for you."

"I never asked you to do that."

"No, you didn't. I did it because we're family. Family does for each other." He thought of the Rockfords, of how different their charmed life was compared to this shitstorm of a situation. "Of course, you never asked me to take the rap for you this time either, just went ahead and planned it that way." His eyes stung with angry tears. He blinked hard and steeled his resolve. "But I won't take the blame this time. I won't throw my life away again, especially not for someone who—"

"Someone who what?" Shane slammed his hands down on the tabletop, the metal from his handcuffs clanging loud in the small room. "Did you ever consider maybe I am the way I am because of you? Ever think of that, Mr. Martyr? Ever think that maybe if you'd been a better brother—"

"Better brother?" Chase didn't even attempt to keep his voice down now. "Jesus Christ, Shane. How the hell could I sacrifice any more for you than I already have, huh? I did the absolute best I could, Shane. But it's time you took responsibility for your actions."

"Fuck you, Chase!"

He stalked to the far corner of the room and took several deep breaths to calm the rage tearing through him. Arguing about things they couldn't change wouldn't help anyone right now. What would help Shane was getting him to turn on Katherine. He glanced back at his brother over his shoulder. Shane sat hunched at the table now, looking sullen and scared and every single one of his twenty-nine years. "Take the plea bargain they'll offer you. It'll reduce your sentence. Don't hold any loyalty for Katherine

Bryant. That viperous bitch will sell you out in a second."

There. He'd said what he'd come to say. Whether Shane took it to heart or not was his choice. Chase started toward the door, but a voice behind him halted his steps.

"You don't have to go yet."

The quiet, plaintive fear in his brother's tone helped Chase's shattered heart to mend a tad. He turned. "Yeah, I do actually. Someone's got to hire you a goddamned lawyer to help you through this mess, bro. And I'm stuck with the job, because for some insane reason I still love you, man."

With that Chase exited, nearly barreling over Troy in the hallway. Thank God the detective didn't say anything about his mushy departure, just stepped aside, a hint of respect mixed with admiration in his eyes.

FIVE DAYS LATER, Shelby lingered over the grave of her father after all the funeral-goers had left. Her head ached and her eyes felt puffy and scratchy from all the tears she'd cried during the funeral. If only Chase had been there to comfort her, to hold her, to tell her everything would be okay no matter what it felt like today....

She sniffled and glanced up to find Blake Rockford nearby, Henry perched on his right shoulder. She sighed and shook her head. "Please don't tell me you want to give him back. We have a strict 'No-Take-Back-sies' policy at Paws and Play."

"What?" Blake scrunched his nose. "No. Henry's not going anywhere." He turned his head to the side and cooed at the iguana. "Are you, boy?"

Shelby smiled as the large lizard snaked his tongue out to flick Blake's cheek. "You like him then, huh?"

"Of course." Blake turned back to her and grinned. "If I'd known it was going to be this much fun terror-izing my brother, Logan, I would've gotten a Henry years ago."

She nodded, squinting into the bright sunshine. "So, why are you here then?"

"I knew your father pretty well, handling his secu-rity for the past few years. I liked him and wanted to pay my respects."

Emotion clogged her throat again and Shelby's eyes welled anew. "I liked him too."

Blake stepped closer and, side by side, they stood in companionable silence in front of her dad's grave, the slight breeze ruffling the trees and the crisp scent of fall in the air.

Finally, Blake sighed. "He didn't do it, you know. Confess, I mean. Chase turned his brother in instead."

"I know." Shelby pulled a tissue from her tiny handbag and dabbed at her cheeks. Chase had texted her and called her pretty much non-stop since the day he'd left her apartment, not to mention the story of the police apprehending the real killers had been plastered all over the news. Still, she wasn't ready to face him again. Not yet. Not after he'd taken her heart and ripped it to shreds. What if he decided he didn't want her after all? She'd survived the pain once. She wasn't sure she could bear it twice. If Dad had been alive, she would've asked him. Or Mom. But both of them were gone now. Gone and she was on her own.

She pressed the tissue tight against her eyes to fight a fresh wave of tears.

"Try not to be too hard on him, okay?" Blake leaned in closer. "He loves you. The decision he made that day was extremely tough. Poor guy thinks he doesn't have a future."

Shelby frowned, staring at the toes of her black pumps. How could Chase not think he had a future? He was smart and funny and handsome and kind and...

"I'm just..." She turned toward Blake only to find him gone.

He loves you...

She loved Chase too.

Problem was, Shelby wasn't sure her battered heart was strong enough to make amends to the man who could break her with one rejection.

21

———

Chase sat on a bench in Bell Park and looked up into the overcast November sky. It had been almost two weeks since they'd arrested Shane and his next hearing was scheduled for the beginning of December. He'd tried numerous times to get in touch with Shelby—text, phone calls, even stopped by Paws and Play once, but nothing.

No response.

He knew better than most that nothing in life was certain, but he'd always harbored a hopeful dream of him and Shelby back together again. He shrugged and lowered his head. Guess he could send that dream to the junk pile like the rest of the life he'd planned before fate and his brother's crimes had changed all that.

The clammy fog chilled him despite the mid-sixties temps and he shoved his hands in the pockets of his denim jacket, brushing against the bag of homemade treats he'd brought for Snickerdoodle—just in case he happened to run into Shelby here or something. As he gazed around the park on this busy Saturday afternoon, however, there were only plenty of young families and older retirees and none of the angelic-faced woman he pictured every night before falling asleep.

Damn. He missed her like crazy.

From the far corner of the park he spotted a flash of toffee-colored brown—the same shade as Snickerdoodle. Nah. He wrinkled his nose and scoffed. Couldn't be. His luck wasn't that great these days.

Then, behind the large brown dog, ran a woman in a pink parka, her blond curls bouncing wildly as she played with her canine companion.

Oh. My. God. It's her. Shelby.

Panic soon overtook his euphoria. Chase didn't want her to think he was some pathetic stalker or something, sitting here every day in the park just hoping for a glimpse of her. He stood and hurried behind a nearby copse of trees just as Shelby and Snickerdoodle neared the bench he'd been sitting on.

Okay. Okay. You can do this. Just be cool, man.

Chase fisted his hand in his pocket and the plastic treat bag crinkled loud.

Snickerdoodle's ears perked in his direction and before he knew it, forty pounds of excited doggy tackled Chase back against the trunk of a tree. Between slobbery kisses, he managed to give the dog a good scratch behind his ears. "How you doing, boy? I've missed you, too. You don't know how much, buddy."

Shelby peeked around the trees, her eyes wide. "Chase. What are you doing here?"

"Oh, um…" He pushed the dog down and straightened his clothes as best he could. "I was, uh, just taking a walk."

"Here?" Her tone matched her incredulous expression. "Blake's house isn't anywhere near here. Snickerdoodle, no. Get over here, boy."

The dog trotted happily to her side, his tongue hanging out and his tail wagging. Chase would've switched places with that mutt in a heartbeat. He pulled the bag of treats from his pocket and handed them to her, avoiding her question. "Here, I got these for him."

"Oh." She took them and after much whining from Snickerdoodle, fed him one. "Uh, thanks."

"You're welcome." They stared at each other in

awkward silence. "So."

"So." Shelby reached down to adjust the dog's leash, bringing her into closer proximity to Chase. Her floral scent drifted to him and his gut clenched tight.

He shuffled his feet. "I've been thinking about getting a pet of my own."

"Yeah?" She glanced up at him, her blue eyes just as bright and beautiful as he'd remembered. "What brought about this decision?"

Tired of holding all his emotional cards so close to the chest, he revealed a little of what he was feeling. "Well, you mentioned once they're a good cure for lonely people."

She straightened, her gaze narrowed. "And you're lonely?"

God, yes. "A little, yeah."

"I see." She tugged Snickerdoodle a bit closer and gave him a second treat to keep him calm. "Stop by the shelter next week. I'll see if we can find someone compatible for you."

I already found someone compatible. He coughed to cover the lump of want now clogging his throat. He wanted to tell Shelby how he felt, but he didn't want to scare her away. Not now, when she was at least talking to him. "Yeah, okay. Sure. I can do that."

"Great." She chewed on her lower lip. "We, uh, we buried my dad last week."

"Oh, right. I read about it in the paper. So sorry I couldn't be there."

"That's all right. It was probably better you weren't, considering everything that happened." She inhaled sharply and looked away. "His death was such a waste. I always knew Katherine was a manipulative, money-hungry bitch, but I never thought she'd actually kill to get what she wanted." She chuckled, an unpleasant sound. "Remember that appointment Katherine said my dad had with his attorney to change the will? Yeah. Found out that was actually to start divorce proceedings. He never would've cut me out of his will. Never. She's such a liar."

"Huh." Chase stepped a little closer to her warmth, encouraged to be back on familiar territory again. "At least that explains why she took such drastic action. With a divorce, she'd get nothing."

"Yep. Not a penny. She wasn't as smart as she thought she was, though."

"Oh really?"

"Nope. She'd lied to the detectives telling them my father planned to change his will and leave everything to her so that it would look like I had motive. Remember how she sent me the fake will? She was probably hoping the police would eventually search my place and find it, but I outsmarted her on that one when I put it into my Dad's safe. I knew she'd been in the safe before and wanted to put it in there just to show her I was on to her, but it turned out to my benefit. The cops eventually looked in the safe and found both the wills. They proved that one to be a fake with Katherine's fingerprints all over it and even matched the ink from the pen she forged my father's signature with to an expensive Chanel pen she had in her purse."

"Good, I'm glad they have another piece of evidence against her. So, I take it she's still locked up, awaiting her arraignment?"

"Couldn't make her bail. Too bad, not sad. Not at all." A small smile formed on Shelby's full lips for the first time since she'd found him hiding behind the trees. He'd do anything to see that smile every day, for the rest of his life. She bent to pet the top of Snicker-doodle's head. "So, what's going on with your brother?"

"Shane?" He gestured toward the bench he'd sat on earlier and they both took a seat. "Well, he took the plea bargain the cops offered, and the attorney I hired got his sentence reduced. He ratted out Katherine, so with any luck, he won't be in prison long, given that Katherine was the real brains behind it all."

"That's good." She crossed her legs toward him and her knee brushed his. He did his best to ignore the electric tingle now zinging through his system from the brief contact and instead concentrated on what she was saying, or at least tried to. "So do you know what kind of pet you want?"

"Huh? Oh, a dog. Yeah definitely a dog." Her knee bumped his again, but this time she didn't pull away, making him a bit braver. "Do you have one like Snickerdoodle?"

She tilted her head to the side. "I have a fluffy white shit-zhu and a black Pomeranian. But I'd have to make sure you'd provide a suitable home first."

"Frou-frou dogs." His gaze dropped to her lips before returning to her eyes. "I could come check them out. Then if I like one, you could check me out to see if I'm suitable. No obligation, of course."

Pretty pink color flooded her cheeks and she scooted closer. "What if I want an obligation?"

"Excuse me?" Snickerdoodle nuzzled his head into Chase's lap, distracting him. She couldn't have meant what he wanted her to mean, could she? "I'm sorry. Could you repeat that?"

"I said." She took his hand. "What if I want an obligation? From you."

Nope. No mistaking her touch, or that look in her eyes. His heart kickstarted then beat triple time. *Don't blow this, buddy. Don't expect too much, too soon. Don't...* He severed the negative track looping in his head and for the first time in such a long time, let hope take the wheel.

Chase laced his fingers with hers then brushed a soft kiss over her knuckles. "What kind of an obligation?"

"Well, let's see." She snuggled into his side. "How about you adopt a dog from my shelter and something else."

"Something else?" The way she was nuzzling the side of his neck made him crazy. He shook his head to clear the warm fuzzies clouding his brain. "What something?"

"Me."

His breath hitched. "You?"

"Mmm hmm." She met his gaze, her lips hovering close to his. "If you still want me."

Her lips were on his before he noticed her move. When they broke apart, his fingers were tangled in her curls and her face was flushed and he'd never seen a more beautiful sight in all his life. His words emerged rough. "Does that answer your question?"

"I believe it does, yes."

Chase laughed, the sound bursting from him with all the joy now filling his heart.

Shelby cupped his cheeks and rubbed noses with him. "Just don't ever leave me like that again, okay?"

"Never." He kissed her again, this one full of love and hope and possession. "That last time damned near killed me."

"Me too."

Apparently tired of being ignored, Snickerdoodle jumped up and burrowed between them, effectively ending their romantic interlude, at least for the time being.

Shelby laughed and hugged the dog tight. "I think he missed you too."

"I missed both of you." He scratched the dog under the chin then put his arm around Shelby and kept her as close as their awkward position would allow. "And I'm not going anywhere. Not again. No matter what, you're stuck with me."

"Good." Shelby leaned over and he met her halfway in a quick peck on the lips.

"Good."

As if in agreement, Snickerdoodle woofed loud as his wagging tail beat back and forth between them.

****

WANT MORE ROCKFORDS?

The only thing keeping Whistleblower Alison James alive is her uncanny ability with numbers. Unfortunately it's also why she's being hunted. Can the Rockfords help? Read the next book in the Rockford Series today:

NO TIME TO RUN

JOIN my readers list to get new release notifications:
http://ladobbs.com/newsletter

DID you know that I write mysteries under other names? Join the LDobbs reader group on Facebook and find out! It's a fun group where I give out inside scoops on my books and we talk about reading!
https://www.facebook.com/groups/ldobbsreaders

ALSO BY L. A. DOBBS

Sam Mason Mysteries

***

Telling Lies (Book 1)

Keeping Secrets (Book 2)

Exposing Truths (Book 3)

Betraying Trust (Book 4)

Killing Dreams (Book 5)

More books in the Rockford Security Series:

Cold As Her Heart

A Game of Kill

No One To Trust

No Time To Run

Don't Fear The Truth

Hide From The Past

ABOUT THE AUTHOR

L. A. Dobbs also writes light mysteries as USA Today Bestselling author Leighann Dobbs. Lee has had a passion for reading since she was old enough to hold a book, but she didn't put pen to paper until much later in life. After a twenty-year career as a software engineer, she realized you can't make a living reading books, so she tried her hand at writing them and discovered she had a passion for that, too! She lives in New Hampshire with her husband, Bruce, their trusty Chihuahua mix, Mojo, and beautiful rescue cat, Kitty.

Her book "Dead Wrong" won the "Best Mystery Romance" award at the 2014 Indie Romance Convention.

Her book "Ghostly Paws" was the 2015 Chanticleer Mystery & Mayhem First Place category winner in the Animal Mystery category.

Join her VIP Readers group on Facebook:

https://www.facebook.com/groups/ldobbsreaders

Find out about her L. A. Dobbs Mysteries at:

http://www.ladobbs.com

9 781946 944696